Children's Literature

Amanda's Choice

By the same author

CECILY

Amanda's Choice

Isabelle Holland

J. B. LIPPINCOTT COMPANY
Philadelphia   New York

Amanda's Choice

chapter one

"You'd better know what you're doing," Amanda said, putting a leg over the banisters. "My father's a very important man."

"Yeah."

Her mother, Amanda reflected, had always said that people who said "yeah" were common. But her mother was a fine one to talk. Besides which, she was dead. The thought cost Amanda no pang at all, or very little. She was quite sure her mother had never liked her and, to be fair, hadn't pretended to, much. And Amanda had fully returned her lack of interest.

Still and all, the dark young man in his dirty T-shirt and stained jeans was certainly no Ivy League princeling. In her twelve years Amanda had seen the denizens of the better eastern colleges troop in and out of the Big House

and the guest cottage in the wake of her two older half
brothers and half sister. They might affect old jeans and
filthy sneakers. They might even sprout hair on the face
and down the neck. But they still didn't look like this—this
weirdo, with his beat-up face. She eyed him over her
bubble gum, crossed her eyes to see if she could make the
gum balloon out again, found she couldn't and sucked it
back in.

She shifted the wad. "Why's the old man letting you have
the cottage? You a writer or something? Is he on that kick
again?"

He straightened up from the carton of books he was
unpacking. "Look, kid, why don't you blow—go play dolls
or witches or whatever you play? You shouldn't be here,
anyway."

"Why not?" She put as much insolence as she could in
the question. "It's gonna be mine when I'm twenty-one.
Mother left it to me. My father can only use it until then
and then I'll use it." This was an old anger. She watched
him reach up to the shelf with a handful of books and then
bend down again for some more from the carton. As though
he owned the place. "I'll bet you're not even gonna pay
rent. You're just mooching." Casually she extracted her
gum. Necessity had forced her to chew it a long time since
she'd forgotten to bring any fresh, and it was fragmented.
Pushing a grubby finger in her mouth, she groped around
her teeth, pulled some gummy bits out and wiped them on
her shorts.

He caught the movement. "Make yourself at home," he
said sarcastically.

From one of her brothers' friends she might have taken
it. Might. But not from this one.

She pulled a phrase from the past, lengthening her upper
lip, pulling her brows up and her lids down. "Keep a civil

tongue in your head." It sounded corny but grand. The
highborn lady throwing out the nervy lowborn suitor. And
lowborn was the word for this one. She could almost hear
her mother pronounce the words.

He straightened from the carton and looked at her for a
minute. There was something about his face that made her
sit very still on the banister rail. It was not only coarse and
ugly, she decided. It was mean. Then he moved toward her.

She tried to jump down, but something froze her. He
stopped in front of her. "I said blow. Now get out."

"I'll go when I—" she started in a high squeak, but she
didn't finish. He jerked her down and frog-marched her
to the door.

"And don't come back."

And then it hit: blind rage. Turning, she threw up her
skinny arms and pushed his out. He was a big young man
with thick muscles, but she caught him by surprise. His
grip loosened and she kicked out and up, the way she'd
overheard her half sister and her giggling friends discuss
how a girl could take care of herself. Unfortunately—or
fortunately—she missed.

The next thing she knew she was outside the front door,
which he had slammed behind her.

But she had a carrying voice with a load of hate behind
it. Despite all her many governesses' best efforts, she had
learned one or two phrases here and there, and she used
them now.

But nothing happened. Either he was deaf or he didn't
care. After a while her rage wore itself out, along with the
paint on the door, which she had kicked. "You stupid jerk,
you creep," she screamed hoarsely as a parting endearment.
But the steam had gone out of her. Now all she felt was sick.

"Amanda."

She turned. What with the commotion she was making,

she hadn't heard the doctor's car drive up. He was the town doctor, the general practitioner for the Island. Amanda, who had been a subject of interest to some of the best clinicians, specialists and psychiatrists in the northeastern seaboard, despised GP's as a matter of course. But she had sometimes found it difficult to despise Dr. Townsend. He might be old, crumpled and (by the standards of her family, anyway,) poor. But there was something about him and his voice that had always kept her from expressing some of the juicier sentiments on her mind. Instead, she glared at him, her tawny eyes narrow in her unappealing face.

"Want a lift?" he asked.

"No."

He put the car in gear. "Suit yourself. But it's going to rain."

Amanda put her tongue out in an experimental way.

His hand on the gear, the doctor looked at her. "Just out of curiosity, why do you do that?"

"Because you're a pig."

Despite himself and long experience, he was annoyed to feel a prod of anger. In some way that he couldn't account for she had the faculty of stinging. "You'd deserve it if I got out of the car and gave you a good spanking."

She looked almost pleased. "I'd scream and scream and scream—"

"Nobody'd hear you."

"—and then I'd go up to the house and scream until Miss Cathaway would have to call New York, to the psychiatrist, and then they'd have to get my father and he'd have to fly home and when he got here he'd be mad and I'd tell him how you beat me and hurt me and did wrong things to me, and he'd be so mad he'd chase you out of the village and have you unfrocked and you'd never get another job and people would laugh at you."

Despite his irritation his mouth twitched. "You don't unfrock a doctor, Amanda. If you're going to make threats you should learn the proper words."

He was laughing at her! Amanda's face went crimson. Stooping down, she picked up one of the numerous jagged stones that littered the Island, giving it its name—Stone Island. So help me, the doctor thought, she's going to throw it at me.

She did. It missed his head but struck the car window behind. The glass cracked. "Amanda—"

She was already stooping for another rock. Quickly he got out of the car. She hurled the stone as he came toward her. Fortunately, she was neither accurate nor strong. It glanced off his shoulder. Amanda's fits of rage had become notorious on the Island. But this was the first time the doctor had actually seen one. His face showed shock and horror. "Listen to me, Amanda—"

He reached out and got her by the shoulders, but with amazing strength she twisted away, screamed an unprintable epithet at him, and ran off.

When the stitch in her side became painful, Amanda stopped running and threw herself down onto the scrubby grass. Her heart thudded against her rib cage and she sucked in her breath in long gasps. As her breath eased, she realized her rage had diminished—had gone back in the house, as she sometimes thought of it. Because she thought of it as a living Thing somewhere in the region of her stomach that, once started, had to keep on pressing out until it burst from her as though it were a tree. It was terrible when it started and she could feel the tearing inside her. But it was awful in a different way when it went back inside, because then she was alone with what she had done and with the memory of the faces she'd done it in front of, who were hating her or despising her or telling her father. And he was looking at her in the way he sometimes had, as though she weren't there at all.

Scowling, she sat up and dug her fingers into the turf, tearing at the grass. Because she had successfully thwarted Miss Cathaway's efforts to make her take a bath both last night and this morning, she looked slightly dirty all over, most notably her hands, feet, and neck. Her shorts and cotton-knit shirt were stained.

Her father. Robert Stewart Hamilton.

The thought of him made the pressing inside her start to push out again. Putting a grubby hand on her midriff, she pushed in, hoping it would loosen the pressure. But it was the wrong thing to do. Quite suddenly she was sick, just barely managing not to get it on her front. Bending over she heaved and spat on the grass.

Son of a skunk, she said aloud, and felt slightly better. Son-of-a-skunk, son-of-a-skunk, Robert Stewart Son-of-a-skunk. Lying back, she stared up at the gray-blue sky and sang it softly to herself. Lousy stinking son-of-a-skunk. The rhythm soothed her. She stretched her arms upward. *Leave your supper and leave your sleep . . . and join your play-fellows in the street. . . .* The music in her head stopped. She sat up and stared at her ankles. That jerk down in the cottage. Her father had promised her he would keep the cottage vacant this summer, so that it could be hers, a place she could go to, to get away from Miss Cathaway. He had promised. . . . Just like he had promised to take her out on the boat, only he took that woman who had dropped in, instead. Just like he'd promised her a pony, only after the puppy—

Quickly she jumped up and started to run up the hill, the verse mocking through her head, keeping time to her feet:

Boys and girls come out to play,
The moon doth shine as bright as day.
Leave your supper and leave your sleep,
And join your playfellows in the street.

Square. Mother Goose. Garbage. But the picture from
the book, the one that her old nurse, Bridie, used to read to
her swam in front of her eyes. There was the colored page
showing the houses with peaked roofs bending toward each
other, and the strange light streaming down from the moon,
and all the children in odd clothes, coming from everywhere, greeting one another in the streets of the old town,
and dancing, as though they had taken the town and it was
theirs.

She stopped at the path leading from the pines to listen.
Was anyone coming from the Big House? She heard a car
door slam and waited. But there was no sound of an engine.
Who would be visiting there now? The doctor, of course.
A chill went through her. He was on his way up when she
saw him. He had looked at her as though he thought she
were nuts. He would probably report to Miss Cathaway
what she'd said and that she put her tongue out. And they
would agree that she should be sent to a special school, like
that last nurse, Obnoxious O'Reilly, said. Irish cow.

Amanda paused, waiting for some kind of satisfaction to
come from the words, like an incantation. But the magic
didn't work this time. She ran to the top of the cliff and
looked down. The rocks below were like gray molars. To
her left the cliff curved back, revealing, down below, a
pebbly beach, a wooden jetty and a boathouse, now empty.
Once it had been the home of the *Pied Piper* the boat her
father and The Three—her two half brothers and half
sister—used to sail, summer after summer.

Lying on her stomach, Amanda stared at the foam creep-
ing around the jetty pylons and the beach. Two memories,

clear as movies, pushed to the surface. Both hurt, but she couldn't stop them:

The first was a summer five or six years ago, when her mother was alive. The Three were home: Buzz, her older half brother who was eighteen, and the twins, Chuck and Giselle, sixteen. It was the first time that summer that they were going out on the *Pied Piper*. Amanda was on the lawn, sloping down the other side toward the jetty, watching them laughing and horsing around. They locked arms around their shoulders, bent three blond heads, and chanted solemnly, moving in a circle, voices spooky:

> *In thunder, lightning or in rain,*
> *When shall we three meet again?*

Amanda ran down the lawn and cliff path and jumped onto the jetty. "Four, four," she yelled, ducking under their arms, trying to get her head under Buzz's shoulder.

"Beat it, kid," he said.

Her father, on the boat, was struggling with the mainsail. "For God's sake, let her play with you. Nobody else will play with her."

"You blame them?" That was Chuck, grinning.

Her father looked up at the sky. "Better go on back, Amanda. We're going out and it's going to be rough."

But she was trying to climb on the boat. "Let me go. I want to go, too."

"You'll get seasick and upchuck all over the boat like last time," Buzz said.

Her father lifted her back onto the dock. "We'll take you out when it's calmer. Run on back. Your mother's on the porch."

"You're just not the seagoing type, kid," said Giselle, who was. She was pulling up the jib, long legs braced on the deck of the *Pied Piper*, blond hair caught together in back with a blue scarf.

"I want to go. . . ."

"For crying out loud—"

But it wasn't her father who picked up her writhing body. It was the twins, Chuck and Giselle, laughing, one at each end so she couldn't kick or bite, stronger than she, relentlessly carrying her up the long green lawn to the house. . . .

"Where'll we put her, Cynthia?" They asked the dark, sophisticated woman sitting there in tailored slacks, holding a drink.

Her mother's voice was cool and amused. "Take her upstairs to Bridie. I really can't have her littering up the porch. The Griffins are coming for cocktails."

That was when she had really started to struggle. But it did no good. She was screaming when they lugged her upstairs. "She's all yours," they said to Bridie in the playroom, and pitched her in.

She went on screaming until Bridie slapped her. Then Bridie's arms were around her, her soft bosom under Amanda's cheek, her voice gentle and soothing. The hysterical sobbing calmed, but between hiccoughs Amanda threw up once or twice, so Bridie put her to bed and sat beside it, with Amanda clinging to her hand, murmuring in her rich lilt, *No, darling, I'll not be leaving you. . . .*

But Bridie—like everyone else—lied. She married and left.

There had been many governesses after Bridie, sandwiched between different schools in New York where the Hamiltons lived in the winter. Then, about a year later, her mother left. One day she came downstairs with her suitcase, kissed Amanda on the cheek, told her to try for once to be a good girl, and walked out the front door. She never came back. Sometime after that—perhaps another year—Amanda learned from her father that her mother had been killed in an automobile accident. There were more governesses. That Thing came bursting out of Amanda more and more often. The governesses, one after the other, kept marching downstairs, hats on, and out the front door. And with each departure her father got less and less patient. Then, six months ago, there was Nurse O'Reilly. And right from the beginning she was trouble.

Nurse O'Reilly had authority. She wore starched white and she talked all the time about The Clinic. After the second or third battle with Amanda, she started talking about a Special School for Disturbed Children, and, what was worse, she talked about the school to Amanda's father. And Robert Hamilton, who said he was tired of the fights and the fusses and the continual uproar that greeted him when he came home at night or was back from one of his many trips, listened.

This led to the other painful memory that happened only two months ago, right after Nurse O'Reilly had slammed on *her* hat and left, still talking about the Special School. They were on the Island then, for the summer. Amanda's father had come up from New York to see her, and to tell her that he had made arrangements for her to go to That School.

"What kind of a school?" Amanda said, although she was pretty sure she knew.

He hesitated. "A special school, Amanda, one that is for girls with—problems."

"I don't have any problems."

"You act as if you do."

"Only because—"

"Because what?"

"Because everybody's so stupid." It was the wrong thing to say. But there was no right thing.

He sat down. They were in the playroom and he looked huge in the small chairs there. "Amanda, when everybody's wrong, it's time you thought about maybe it's you. Everybody can't be wrong."

"Why not?" She said. For a moment there she had thought he might put his arms around her and hold her on his lap the way he used to—sometimes—when she was little.

Instead, he sighed and got up. "Just because they can't. Just the fact that you think the way you do makes me think this school is right for you."

"And if I say I'm wrong, then you'd send me anyway."

He frowned. "Maybe not. Maybe if you ever admitted you were wrong or naughty I'd know—"

Nervously, while he was talking, she scraped back her hair.

He broke off. "Amanda—" He sounded exasperated. "Don't you ever wash your hands? Doesn't—didn't—Nurse O'Reilly tell you little girls should at least be clean? God knows I don't expect you to act like something out of *Little Women*, but I'm sure your governess—"

"She didn't tell me anything."

She saw him frown, making the lines in his face deep. He rubbed the bridge of his nose with his knuckle, a habit he had when he was worried. "That's a lie, Amanda. I've heard her."

"She does it around you. Not other times."

His frown hardened. "You're not telling the truth, Amanda. About Miss O'Reilly. The trouble was you couldn't pull the wool over her eyes the way you did the others. She was a conscientious woman. I can't imagine that she didn't try to make you behave, dress properly, and bathe. And now she's gone, I really have no choice but to—"

She could feel it starting, the pain inside. But with all her strength she held it, as her father's voice went on and on, hating her, scolding her, wanting her not to be his daughter, wanting her not to be. Because if she let go, for a second, if she let him see the way she felt, he would send her from the Island. He would send her to That School. So she put her head down in her arms and cried. He stopped then and after a while he went away and back to New York.

Each day for a week she waited for the mail with windmills in her stomach, sure her father would write saying he was coming to pick her up and take her to That School. But, strangely, he didn't. Instead, he wrote saying that a Miss Patience Cathaway (what a name! she thought, reading the letter) would shortly be arriving *and that this was absolutely her last chance* (underlined). That Miss Cathaway had been recommended by a cousin of the rector of their church in New York. That Amanda might find her easier to get along with because she was not a trained nurse or real governess and didn't have the rigidity that nurses sometimes had. But that if she didn't obey Miss Cathaway, if he had any reports of trouble, he would put her in That School with no ifs, ands or buts. . . .

He didn't even say he was sorry he couldn't come up. Even though by then it was late June and always, always before, when The Three were home from school, from camp, from college, from the army, from Europe, from wherever they had been, he would come up to the Island in June and spend July there. . . .

Now July was almost gone.

Amanda turned over in the grass and stared at the cloud

puffs that sailed above her. Maybe her father would come
in August. He hadn't actually said he wouldn't come.

Old Cathy had turned out to be a bore and a drag with
her *How's about us doing this?* and *Why don't you and I
do that?*, so cozy and palsy-walsy she made Amanda want
to throw up. But if her father might come in August, she'd
better mind her manners and cool it, not only with Un-
speakable Cathy, but with that jerk down at the cottage. . . .

"How's Amanda behaving?" The doctor asked Miss
Cathaway up at the Big House. He had just lanced a
carbuncle for Mrs. Little, the Hamiltons' housekeeper, and
was now on his way out accompanied by the governess.

He started across the polished boards and rag rugs
toward the front door. One of the nice things about this
house was the light that streamed through its windows on
every side and through the fine fanlight over the door.

"Oh—she seems to be adjusting. She's out a lot, I don't
try to keep too close a rein on her. I think children
shouldn't be repressed too much, don't you, Doctor?"

A vision of the protruding tongue and the hate-filled
little face flickered across his mind. "I wouldn't call
Amanda repressed, whatever else she is." He paused, hand
on the doorknob. "In fact, I think some repression would
do her a world of good and make life more comfortable
for the rest of us."

"Do you really think so?" asked Miss Cathaway anx-
iously. Her eyes strayed to the hall table where a letter was
lying. "She got a letter from her father this morning. I do
hope it makes her happy. Sometimes—" her voice broke off.
She looked more bewildered than ever.

"Sometimes?" the doctor repeated gently.

"I don't know whether she adores or detests him. Every
day she asks if there's a letter for her. Once I asked her

who she was expecting to hear from and she said, 'My father, of course, stupid.'" The governess sighed. "I suppose I should have reprimanded her for speaking to me like that. But I think respect has to be earned, don't you?"

"I do. But I don't think letting her trample all over you is the way to do it. Amanda needs someone who'll stand up to her. It's a pity her father isn't around more—" He broke off. "Here she comes now."

Miss Cathaway peered around the door. "Amanda, there's a letter from your father."

Amanda, who was strolling across the driveway, paused and then leaped onto the porch. Without so much as a glance or a "by your leave," she pushed between the doctor and Miss Cathaway.

"Amanda," Miss Cathaway started.

But Amanda, ripping open her letter, had walked to the other end of the room.

"Don't waste your breath," the doctor said drily. "Just hope it puts her in a good mood." He gave Miss Cathaway's hand a brief pat. "And stop looking like that."

"Like what?"

"Like an early Christian waiting for her lion."

Miss Cathaway laughed, closed the door and, after a glance at Amanda's back and bent head, went upstairs.

The envelope was one of the long office ones, and the address was typed, so her father's secretary, Miss Petersen, must have done that. But inside, on memo paper, was a letter in his handwriting, sloping, uneven and hurried:

. . . I know I said I thought the guest house would be vacant this summer, but this is a young man who needs a quiet place to work, and I think, Amanda, it's time you realized that other people in the world don't have your advantages. If he weren't there he'd have to be in a hot

*tenement in a noisy street in New York—not very helpful
to someone trying to compose an opera, would you say?
So try to see things from his point of view. That's what
life is about, seeing things from other people's point of view,
and it's something you've never done, which worries me
very much. Those of us who were born with more than
our share of the goods of this world must give more, and
you're not too young to learn this. It's always distressed
me that you don't seem to have any concept of this at all.*

Something was crossed out then. Amanda put it up to
the light and slowly spelled out the words. . . . *The
others had it from the beginning* underneath the heavy
cross marks of his stub pen. Obviously he'd thought better
of that, but she felt the hot anger begin in her anyway.
. . . The letter picked up, *so stay out of his way. He's
had a difficult time, lately, and people bother him. Let him
have the summer in peace and quiet and maybe things will
work out for him. So be my grown-up, considerate girl
and give the guest cottage a wide berth.*

She put the letter down, the anger pushed aside by a
pleasant feeling brought on by the words, *my grown-up,
considerate girl.* My grown-up, considerate girl . . .

She went back to the letter. *It looks like I won't get to
the Island until late August, if then. The twins are in France
and Germany, and since I have to go there anyway on
business, I might as well take my vacation there and go
and see. . . .*

It was like a trapdoor, the sudden feeling. Everything
dropped. The house was silent, the clock tingled, shuddered
and struck. *If then . . .*

Numbly she raised the sheet of paper again . . . *but I
know you'll have a good time because you love being on
the Island, and I think you'll find Miss Cathaway much
easier on you than—*

She tore it again and again and again and threw the pieces all over the floor and rugs.

Mrs. Little, her hand held protectively over the carbuncle on her side, came in. "Pick up those pieces this minute, Amanda!"

"You fat cow, you stink," Amanda shrieked. Then she ran out of the front door and slammed it after her. One of the glass panes shattered onto the floor.

chapter two

There was a way into the cottage other than the conventional ones by the two doors. Up the stone wall, up the tree, crawl along the branch, catch hold of the edge of the roof, along the gutter, and into the attic window.

Amanda jumped lightly onto the floor. The familiar, smell surrounded her: dust, mothballs, old books, old wood. She stood poised for a second, listening. But the floor, built originally to hold up several tons of hay, was thick and solid. No sound came up. By the same token, no sound would go down.

Nevertheless she trod lightly over the long low room to the little bed under the window on the other side. Fortunately, the floor was covered with one of the many carpets that had been declared too threadbare for downstairs use or use in the Big House.

Amanda eased onto the little bed. Its ancient springs creaked. It was an old iron cot, really. And there was no real reason it had not been sold or given away with the rest of the annual shipment to the Salvation Army. But it had been relegated to the attic and forgotten.

Covering it was an old, red bedspread, and under that an equally old eiderdown, so that it was soft. The pillow had been her own addition, stolen from her bedroom up at the Big House. She had placed it at the foot of the bed so that lying down, her face looking out the window, she could see the edge of the cliffs and beyond that, the gray sea.

She lay down now, watching the white edges slide toward her, break, and reform. The sky was gray, too, but there was a hard line at the horizon, where the much darker gray of the ocean began.

For a long while she lay there, watching the waves change and shift, masses of them, like soldiers on a battlefield. Slowly the sky grew darker. Without consciously crossing any line of mood she started to cry, only really aware of the fact when the tears wet the rough stitching of the bedspread under her cheek. It was getting dark. At the extreme edge of her vision, where the coast of the mainland curved outward, she saw a few lights come on, looking, somehow, lonely instead of cozy.

Footsteps sounded on the staircase. She stiffened, waiting to hear them on the uncarpeted stairs outside the door, but they stopped on the second-floor landing and walked in her direction underneath her. The night outside leapt into darkness as the light blazed from the window beneath.

"Stink," Amanda said quietly to herself. Wiping her face, she got up and tiptoed across the room to the window she had entered. Just as she feared. The attic window was above the window of the room downstairs. He had obviously not drawn the blind, because the light threw the trunk of her tree into vivid relief. It would be better to wait until he'd gone downstairs again. But it was late. The gray of the sky was now almost black. If she weren't back, that idiot Cathaway would start fussing. Sooner or later someone would come down to the cottage. They always looked for her there when they couldn't find her anywhere else. That mustn't happen. Not because of the scolding, which she was indifferent to. Nor because she feared a spanking—no one had spanked her since Bridie, who used to spank her regularly, quite unknown to Amanda's parents.

But if someone came down to the cottage and they searched the attic, they would find out how she came in, and that was something that no one, so far, knew. Once they discovered that, the creep downstairs could lock the window, her private entrance.

Amanda paused, one knee on the windowsill. If she went down the tree he would see her. If she didn't, they'd come from the Big House. Neither was any good. She'd have to do something else.

Letting herself lightly back onto the floor she stood in the middle of the floor and thought. The only thing to do was to go down the inside staircase, now, while he was in the bedroom, and let herself quietly out the front or the back door.

Fortunately, she had on sneakers that made almost no noise on the wooden steps. Unfortunately, she tripped over her own shoelace when she was safely running down the carpeted flight leading to the living room. The floor below seemed to rise to greet her; she became aware of the red thread running through the rag rug below. Almost slowly, she made a grab at the banister. Her nails grazed the polished wood. She heard a voice cry out and then her shoulder hit the wall and she plunged down. All she could think of was the noise she was making.

The pain was terrible, not being able to take a breath. Panic-stricken, she pulled in and felt a tremendous thump on the back, followed by another one even harder. He's beating me, she thought, outraged. But the thump must have worked, because suddenly, in blind relief, she felt air come into her lungs.

She was looped over his knee. He was pounding her back. After he could see she was breathing he jerked her up.

"Just what the blazes are you doing here? I told you to beat it."

His anger hit her like a blow. She could see it in his face, his eyes, and she could feel it emanating from him. His hand went back and she instinctively crouched. But he was holding her with the other. Then he lowered it, took hold of her with both hands and shook her so that she went back and forward like a doll. "If you ever do that again I'll beat you until you won't know what hit you. Don't you ever come sneaking in like that again. How did you get in, anyway? I thought I had both doors locked."

His eyes were as black as puddles of tar; the skin, pulled tight over his thin face, sallow.

"Leave me alone, you louse," she shrieked. "If my father knew you were hitting me he'd come back and kill you."

It would be marvelous if it were true. But he didn't know it wasn't. "He'd kill you," she said again.

"Yeah! I bet. He told me not to let you get in my hair. He said you could be a damn nuisance. He was right. I don't want you here. Now get out and stay out."

He was not shaking her anymore but was holding her, and the mean expression was on his face.

"You're lying. You've never talked to my father."

It had just been something to say, but she saw at once that she was right. "You're making it up." She watched his face and pressed home her advantage. "I bet you aren't even supposed to be here."

"Well, you're wrong. Maybe I haven't talked to your father. But he wrote me and his lawyer gave me the keys to the house."

She remembered then her father's letter. Obviously he did intend for the young man to be here.

"What's your name?" she said, hoping he'd forget he was holding her and let go.

But he didn't. Instead, his hands closed more tightly on her skinny arms.

"Ouch! You're hurting me. You big bully."

"I told you. I don't want you around here. Maybe if I hurt you a little you won't come back."

He really was hurting her, and something—some anger— in his eyes frightened her. "If you hurt me I'll show the doctor and he'll have to write my father and no matter what anybody said to you they'll have to throw you out! LET GO."

For a second she thought it wouldn't work and got badly scared. But his hands loosened. "Just so you stay out of my way."

She rubbed her arms. He leaned back against the banisters. They glared at each other.

There were several things she'd like to do, but she recognized that they were at an impasse. She could get him thrown out, all right. But he could get her sent to That School.

His skin was not only sallow, it was pitted, as though he'd had chicken pox. He had a curved, bony Roman nose. He also had several scars: one ran down his cheek,

another across his neck, and a third went up into the thick
black curly hair. He looked like a small-time hood straight
out of the movies.

Furious, because she felt helpless, she repeated her question. "What's your name?"

"What's it to you? You won't be using it."

"Look. When I want to come here I'll come. Maybe
you can get me thrown out. But you push me around too
much and I can get you thrown out."

He stared at her silently. "Malcolm Sanderson," he said
finally.

She turned, kicking the rug, and walked slowly into the
room. He had lit a fire in the big stone fireplace, and it
crackled around the logs, filling the room with a coppery
light. The only other light came from a reading lamp near
the wing chair. The curtains were drawn. There was a
glass on the table by the chair, filmed white, as though it
had contained milk. Amanda was suddenly aware of hunger
and of her dinner. But she didn't want to go back to the
house. She wanted to sit here by the fire and drink a glass
of milk and eat some cookies. But he wouldn't let her stay,
and if she did—

On her slow way out the door she stopped by the baby
grand piano that sat across one corner. It had belonged to
her mother. Sheets of lined paper were strewn all over it.

"Father said you were making an opera. It that true?"
She put out a hand.

"Leave that alone." He spoke sharply and moved rapidly
toward her. She skipped out of the way and headed toward
the door. No use to push him too far.

"Just keep your hands to yourself," she said airily, and
opened the front door.

"*Amanda*—" That would be Miss Cathaway, screeching

away up there on the hill. "Amanda, where are you? It's time for dinner."

He grinned suddenly, showing crooked teeth. "I'll tell her you're here." He drew in a deep breath.

"Don't bother," Amanda said, angry that he should end up the victor in this encounter. She would see to it that the odds were evened. Sticking her thumbs in the corner of her mouth, she pulled it into a grimace, crossed her eyes, and stuck out her tongue.

"That's better. Now you're almost pretty."

The door slammed as she aimed a kick at it.

He stood with his back to the door, feeling the thump as her sneaker struck the door. Little hellcat. Like the kids back home. A rancorous anger filled him as he thought of that. Born at the top. All the money in the world. A huge house, one of those fancy governesses, probably a pony, and she was no better than the kids back on the teeming, tenement-littered block on which he had grown up. The only difference was the voice and accent. But for all the plummy tones and broad a's, the dirty little words were the same, and bar a certain way she had of holding her head and of walking, she didn't even look that different. Pick her up, shorts, dirty shirt and all, put her down in the middle of his street, and she'd feel right at home.

He grinned, and then his smile faded, leaving his thin face scowling. It was true that Hamilton's lawyer had given him permission to use the cottage and the keys. His teacher at the conservatory had fixed that, Hamilton being on the Board and a sort of a patron. His teacher hadn't known about that last trouble he'd been in. But being up here would take the heat off. And with the Prof. away himself in Europe, nobody'd know where to find him. By the time the fall came, maybe they'd be busy with something else, and even if they weren't, the Professor would go to bat for him. Malcolm grinned again: he could just hear his teacher—bad environment, broken home, our debt to the deprived—the whole bit.

Malcolm walked toward the fire, his grin broadening. There was nothing in the world that gave him quite the same pleasure as watching the guilt-stricken face of his kindly professor, beating himself for having lived a blameless life, ready to fight anyone who even suggested that a nineteen-year-old boy, however bright, however deprived, is (to quote the priest up at St. Mary of Guadaloupe and, for that matter, his own mother) to a large degree responsible for what he does. It was beautiful. You just fed 'em the right garbage and out it came.

He stood in front of the big chimney piece, and pushed a log with his sneaker. And the Prof. was right. The ones who had everything owed him something. He looked around the room. Everything in it spelled money. He'd been around long enough, had been in the houses of enough of his classmates, to know the difference between old and new money, to know that the simple furniture, the rag rugs and white paneling concealed more real capital than the fancy furnishings and wall-to-wall luxury of the newly rich.

A resentment almost as old as he was tightened his stomach and sent a taste of bile into his mouth. Hate was the only bridge between this world and his own, between the rulers who grew up in houses like this and like the mansion at the top of the cliff, and his own people. Malcolm Sanderson. It was a good name. He'd spent a while choosing it. The initials were the same. Everything else was different.

The names, the nationality they implied, thè background they revealed.

When he'd first written it at the top of a piece of sheet music, the Prof. had smiled and said, "Your own name is better." He must have seen the scornful disbelief on his face because he went on, "Believe me, it's now very fashionable to have a name like yours. You'll get much further with it."

He hadn't really believed him. Even so, it didn't matter. In a place like this it was essential to have a name like Malcolm Sanderson. There was an oval mirror over the mantel. He stared into it. He didn't expect them to believe the name, of course. No one with a name like that would have a face like his. They'd know it was phony. The police would know. At that thought the black brows met over the strong nose. He should have picked another name. But it was done now and there was no point in worrying about it.

Strolling over to the piano, he stared at the sheet music on the frame, on the top and on the floor. Stooping, he picked up the latter. After a few moments looking at it, his face changed subtly, losing its guarded, surly expression. Quietly, between his teeth, he began to whistle and then hum. Without thinking, he sat down at the piano, played the chords he had written, played them again, and then went on, improvising, going back, deepening and then playing the whole from the beginning. After a while he stopped playing and picked up his pencil.

chapter three

"Try and drink your milk, Amanda," Miss Cathaway said automatically, and without much hope.

"I don't like milk." Amanda, who had been on the point of picking up the glass, changed the direction of her hand and took, instead, another gingersnap. The trouble was, she wanted the milk and didn't really like gingersnaps. But by admitting either she would lose face. Miss Cathaway didn't approve of gingersnaps—bad for the teeth, she had once said absent-mindedly. Milk, of course, she approved of. Pity it wasn't the other way around, Amanda thought, her unwinking gaze on the governess as she chewed on the crisp, spicey substance. Then she could please her taste and maintain her guerrilla warfare against her governess at the same time. But the sacrifice for her own, unbroken battlefront was worth it. That'd teach her father to leave this namby-pamby, sissy-squishy female with her. Deliberately, she took another gingersnap, and waited to see what Miss Cathaway would do.

Miss Cathaway felt a familiar dread. A long time ago someone had sent her clergyman father some kind of a leaflet on which was printed the statement *The greatest sin is fear*. She had come to believe it. And there was a President's famous statement: *The only thing we have to fear is fear itself*. She could write a composition about that, too. On the whole subject, she thought with dry, if desperate, humor, she was an expert. And there Amanda sat, those tawny, catlike eyes on her as though they were measuring her for some new torment.

A sense of failure, another constant compassion, settled over the governess. "You'll fail," her father had said to her once, during her brief, calamitous attempt to, make her own way in the world. "Then you'll come home. And you'll stay." He'd been right, of course. Every time she looked as though she might pull together the courage to try again, he'd remind her. Later, when her mother was dead and her father retired, there was no need. She had to take care of him. But he'd remind her anyway from time to time, just to keep on top of things.

And she was failing now with Amanda—had been, from the beginning. She should have written to Robert Hamilton and told him. But that, too, would have taken courage, and she always hoped, each day, that she would fall on the formula or the right words that would reach this terrible child. She had been exposed to all the modern pieties that dictated the belief that Amanda's monstrosities sprang from being mishandled and misunderstood. Give her warmth, affection and lenience, she mused—and you'll get your hand bitten off. It would take a can opener to get through to Amanda. She sighed. Now I will tell her that she must have a bath and she'll refuse and probably swear at me. She smells already. It's unhealthy to let yourself get that dirty, but how do I make an agile twelve-year-old climb into an old-fashioned bathtub? She's almost as big as I am, and a lot stronger.

For a moment Miss Cathaway toyed with the thought of soliciting the aid of Mrs. Little, who suffered from no visible neuroticisms and who was more than large enough to cope, single-handed, with Amanda. But she shrank from the admission of failure it would indicate as much as from the force itself. Besides, Mrs. Little had her carbuncle to think about. "Time for a bath, Amanda."

"All right."

Amanda grinned, knowing she had knocked the wind out of Old Cathy. She slid from the table. "You can clean up the bathroom afterwards." She pounded up the stairs.

"Just as you say, mum," muttered the governess, slapping the dishes onto a tray. She carried them out to the kitchen. "I'll never understand that child. Never."

"Now what?" Mrs. Little was sipping some strong tea. The lancing had been painful, and leaning over to pick up the pieces of Amanda's letter from the floor hadn't helped. The pieces were now Scotch-taped together and she was reading the letter.

Miss Cathaway took the dishes over to the sink. "Just that she takes me by surprise. She refuses to do everything I ask to the point where I don't expect anything else. Then when I look for her to refuse doing something, like taking a bath just now, off she goes like a lamb and does it."

Mrs. Little lifted her eyes. "However she does it it won't be lamblike, you can be sure of that." Her attention went back to the letter. "Be my grown-up considerate girl— Listen to that, will you? As though that little she-devil ever considered anyone!"

Miss Cathaway stared at the sheet. "What's that?"

"Mr. Hamilton's letter to Amanda."

"How did you get hold of it?"

"Because she threw the pieces on the floor in front of me. And when I told her to pick them up she called me a fat cow. If I hadn't had an abcess . . ." One large hand crept to her side. Her face was pink with remembered indignation.

A jolt went through Miss Cathaway. In her upbringing, letters were sacrosanct. She opened her mouth, saw Mrs. Little watching her, as if to see what she were going to say, and closed it again. She could almost hear her mother's voice, *that, my dear, is what you get when you hobnob with servants—stealing letters.*

But, she jibed her ghost, *I am a servant.* Less than one, she mentally added, turning and running water over the dishes. No self-respecting servant, certainly not Mrs. Little, would take what she did. They would either have done the job they'd been hired to do—cope with Amanda—or they would have got out.

"What does he say?" she asked, to pay herself out for her snobbery.

"Oh—tells her that he is letting that young feller have the guest cottage and that she's to give it a wide berth. Says he isn't coming until late August, if then."

"Doesn't he usually come here for the summer?"

"Always did."

"It seems hard on Amanda not to come this year."

"Maybe the place has soured on him since her mother ran off with that reporter."

Miss Cathaway swung around. "Ran off? Mrs. Hamilton?"

"Sure. Where've you been? It was all over the papers." Was there a certain satisfaction in Mrs. Little's broad face?

With untypical bluntness Miss Cathaway said, "I thought you liked Mr. Hamilton."

Mrs. Little flushed. "Sure. He's a good man. Done a lot for the people around here." But there was no affection in her voice.

"But you don't like him for that?"

"With all that money he can afford to."

Miss Cathaway's large dark eyes looked at her with surprise. "I suppose I don't have the right independence of character, but I must say I think it would be lovely to be protected like that all the time."

Mrs. Little went back to the letter. "You'd get tired of it."

Miss Cathaway dried and put away the dishes, turning over the conversation in her mind. "I thought the second Mrs. Hamilton was dead," she said finally.

"As a doornail. Crashed in a car on the French coast somewhere. She and that reporter."

"But the first wife is buried here. I've seen it in the family graveyard behind the church."

"That's right." Mrs. Little turned the letter over. "But he wouldn't have had the second one buried here, even if she'd died in bed with twenty reverends bending over her."

"Did they quarrel?"

"Not exactly what you'd call quarrel." The big woman shifted her bulk and temporarily abandoned the letter. "He'd be so angry he could hit her. Probably would have done her good. Who knows? Maybe she would have stayed with him. But the Hamiltons don't hit their women, more's the pity. He'd freeze up like a thousand icebergs. She'd yell and scream and carry on. Particularly when she was drinking. You could hear her all the way down to the cottage. He'd just walk away. Some newspaperman must have heard a rumor about their trouble. They always tried

to print things about 'The Family.' " Miss Cathaway had
noticed from the time she arrived that when the Islanders
talked about The Family they meant only one family—the
Hamiltons. "Anyway, he came snooping up from some
magazine. Next thing you know, off she went with him.
Never saw her again," Mrs. Little finished with relish.

"Oh." It was food for thought. "How long ago was
that?"

Mrs. Little had gone back to the letter. "That she ran
off? About five years ago. Was dead a year later." There
was more than a hint of cause and effect in her voice.

"It must have been very hard on Amanda. It probably
explains why she is the way she is."

"Just like her mother. No good."

"You can't blame the child for the sins of the mother."

Mrs. Little folded up the letter and put it in her pocket.
"Why not? The Bible says you can. Yes, I know it's
supposed to be outmoded, but sometimes I wonder."

Miss Cathaway was about to take strong issue with this
when she felt something drop on her head. She put a
tentative hand up and felt something wet plop onto it.
"The ceiling must be leaking."

"What?" Mrs. Little glanced up. "Holy Jehoshaphat!"

Miss Cathaway looked up and got several more wet
splats on the face. "What . . . ?" She moved away,
rubbing her face with a handkerchief. "What on earth has
happened?"

Mrs. Little creaked to her feet. "Your lamb has probably
left the bathwater running," she said grimly, and moved
with surprising speed to the back staircase leading from the
kitchen. At the bottom step she turned. "What did she say
to you when she went up?"

Miss Cathaway stared at her in consternation. "She said
I could clean up the bathroom."

chapter four

Malcolm Sanderson stood beside the piano, his shoulders hunched, his hands in his pockets. On the holder in front of him were several sheets of music paper, the ruled lines, except for the top two staves, blank. They had been blank for the last three days, though he had spent hours sitting at the keyboard, his hands groping for a line that had driven him crazy running through his head on the way up here, but that he had lost. The torn remains of several sheets lay on the floor, and he had left them there. Ashtrays around the room were brimming. The fire in the hearth was long dead, but the cinders and ashes lay sprawled over the brick. There was a stale odor in the room which was also cold.

After a few minutes he knocked the music off the piano, slammed the top over the keys and moved to the door. He hadn't been out since the mental block hit him, forcing himself to stay inside until, he thought, sooner or later the thaw would set in and he could find the next step of the theme that had been burning in his head for three years—until now. But the block was still there, harder than ever.

He jerked open the door and stared outside. No one had told him how cold it would be, or how damp, or how the fog would come in from the sea at night, so that when he woke up and tried to look out the window, it was like looking into soft mush.

"It is an outrage," one of the social workers used to say in that flutey, phony voice, "that you children have to stay in the city. You should be in the country where you can see the grass and the trees and the water, instead of these hot, noisy streets."

Well, she could have her country with its dripping cold, its fog, its terrible silences and screeching birds at five in the morning. He'd take the trucks and the yowls, human and animal, from the empty lots. At least they were alive.

With an ache in his chest he remembered the chattering voices of his sisters, the fights, his mother's voice, yelling above the others, the smell of cooking, and his ever-present hunger. But all the time he was home he was driven mad by the music in his head that he couldn't write down for lack of space and peace and three breaths' worth of quiet.

"I'll arrange something," the Prof. had said, when, trying to explain why he hadn't been able to work, he told him about the three rooms and eight children, the two radios going at once, the television. . . . And the next thing he knew he was going down town to one of the towering buildings overlooking the Statue of Liberty and a quiet-voiced lawyer was handing him some keys and a ticket. It was the voice that awed him, kept him silent. It was like another language using the same words, like the English movies he had seen. And the Prof. had said that now he could get the first draft of the opera down, enough to enter for that fellowship that would keep him for the next year or so until he finished at the conservatory and maybe take him abroad for a year or two after he graduated.

"A modern *Flying Dutchman*," the Prof. had said, bemused and a little disappointed. "What gave you the idea? It's a little old-fashioned, isn't it? Some of the others are working in the new electronic area. However," he'd added hastily, not wanting to be guilty of thwarting any creative impulse, "it's an interesting idea. Neo-Wagner, I suppose." He sighed. "Bound to happen sometime. What gave you the idea?"

Malcolm hadn't told the truth, of course. That it was the first opera, or even the first piece of serious music, he'd heard. That he might never have known how he felt about music, or have found his way to the conservatory if he had not been delivering that day from the deli to that woman's apartment on a Saturday afternoon. He had heard the notes bellowing out into the hall as soon as he got off the elevator. If she hadn't been so boozed or doped she wouldn't have taken twenty minutes to find her purse, picking things up and putting them down, muttering to herself. And all the while he stood there, listening to the rippling voices, thunderstruck, dazzled, feeling as though some giant hand had ripped off what he had always thought was the ceiling of the world, only to show another world beyond.

When he left he had walked up and down streets, calmly looking for a parked car that was open with the key in the ignition. It didn't take too long. Then he drove it to an alley he knew, turned on the radio, and listened to the rest of the opera. It could have been two hours later or ten. He neither knew nor cared. When he finally got back to the deli he was fired, but it was worth it. He knew then what he wanted and after that managed to steer clear of really bad trouble. He was fifteen. Since then, the music had never entirely left him.

Slowly, pushing his feet in front of him, he left the house. After a while the grass soaked through his sneakers, making his feet wet as well as cold. He could hardly see three feet in front of him, but by this time it was easier to go on than to go back into the cottage with its silent piano. After a while he came, abruptly, to the upper crest of the cliff, and stood, heart beating, realizing how easily he might have walked over. He couldn't see the sea, of course. But he could hear it, the long soft slaps against the sand and rocks and, surrounding it, the huge silence.

He shivered, shifted his feet and felt a crumbling beneath his left sneaker. The whole weight of his body started to plunge and he felt himself falling into the cottony gray void. He heard a voice, his own, shout and knew it to be useless. All other human beings had gone, decamped, leaving him alone in this ghostly universe. Fear became terror as his fingers clawed at passing rocks that slid under his hands and tore his nails from the quick. Life was sweet, he had not known how sweet, until now when he was losing it. A last cry broke from him as something hard and rough crashed into his body.

The fog had lifted. The gray cotton had blown away while he had been unconscious and a pale sun threw a gentle warmth on his shoulders. But despite the warmth, or in contrast to it, he was shivering and became aware slowly, and by degrees, of the scratchiness of whatever he was lying on. He shifted, and pain shot through his left arm, side, and ankle. Gingerly, he eased up a little, turned his head—and looked once more into death.

He was half sitting, half lying in the forked arms of a small tree sticking out of the side of the cliff. Beneath him, the cliff curved in again. Below that, by about a hundred feet, the blue-black water, with its white foam, hissed around the rocks.

If he so much as moved a hand he might upset the precarious balance that kept him in the tree. He closed his eyes to shut out the sickening view falling away under his buttocks and concentrated on remembering the time he had won a buck from Spike by walking on the parapet of the apartment house, twelve storeys above the street. But a street was one thing. That sliding water with those teeth-like rocks was another. Slowly, slowly, he shifted his cramped foot, and again pain shot up his leg into his thigh. He drew in his breath and waited for the worst of it to pass. Now, he told himself, get hold of yourself. You're still alive. *You're still alive.* If you don't blow it, you can stay that way. Think.

He also listened, forcing himself to recognize and mentally label the sounds he heard. The sea, washing against the rocks. Those screeches were from seagulls. That was a boat whistle, way off somewhere. An engine. . . . His heart soared until he realized it was a plane making large, idle loops. Too far up. Anything else? Nothing. Nothing human. That doesn't mean they aren't there. He sucked in his breath. *Madre de Dios, salvame,* he whispered and then launched his voice against the great silence. "Help!" He sounded about as forceful as a kitten. Without thinking, he braced his body and heard, like a cracking whip, one of the branches under him snap. *Oh, my God, I am heartily sorry that I have offended you.* . . . From what boyhood past of Saturday confessions did that spring from? He always went to the priest who insisted they confess in English. The less he'll understand, he had told himself, though it didn't always work out that way. He drew in his breath. "HELP!"

If he didn't attract somebody fast the whole tree would crack under his weight; he could feel the strain of the brittle wood under him. "Hail Mary, full of grace . . ." As he muttered the prayer his mother's voice seemed to come to him through the wind: *Just once, mal muchacho, it won't hurt you to say one decade of the Rosary. Maybe the Holy Virgin will say a good word for you, not that you deserve it.* . . . "Pray for us sinners now and in the hour of our death. . . . Holy Mother—get me out of this. I'll say the Rosary for the rest of my life, I swear, novenas, everything, if you'll just let somebody hear me." He despised himself. He had renounced the superstition of the Church long since. If he was going to die, he should do it with a proud sneer, agnostic to the end. . . .

"Well, well, well."

He recognized the voice before his eyes went up, and he knew that his prayer had been answered, even if it was obvious that the Blessed Virgin was having a little joke at his expense. . . . Of all people on the Island to have heard his cry.

"You sure have got yourself into a mess, haven't you?" Amanda said delightedly. She was lying on her stomach twenty-five feet above him, her chin cupped in her hands.

"Go get help," he said. "This tree's gonna break any minute."

"No, it won't. Not unless you move. If you stay still there's no telling how long it will hold."

"Look, Amanda—"

"Miss Hamilton to you."

It couldn't be true, but it was. Hatred sent a spurt of

determination through him. Just wait until I get out of this, he promised himself, and her. "Go get some help, kid, huh?"

"Why should I?"

"It's the same as murder if you don't. You want to go to jail?"

"Pooh! Nobody'll know I've been here. You'll just fall and bust your neck or you'll starve to death." With outrage he saw that she had pulled a half-eaten apple from somewhere and had started to nibble at it.

"You're some Christian!"

She looked interested. "Do you believe in Christianity?"

"Look—"

She took a last bite and threw the core of the apple over the cliff. It sailed near him and down. He felt his legs begin to shiver again. Amanda licked her fingers. "Because if you do, why don't you try praying? Mr. Bartholomew— that's our rector—says if you really believe when you pray, you'll get what you want."

He mustn't give in. He mustn't plead. He stared up into the face of the enemy and took his silent stand.

"If you were dead I could have the cottage to myself," Amanda said.

The wind was cold, going through his flesh as though it were a veil. Great waves were coming at him, bringing nausea and dizziness. In one wild, weird moment he could smell the hot spices in his mother's kitchen and feel the heat coming through the open window. . . .

"If I go get help can I come to the cottage whenever I like?"

He tightened his lips and concentrated on not feeling sick.

"If I don't get help you'll fall pretty soon. You're looking kinda sick now."

Hatred filled him, for her and for everything she represented: her family, her money, the way she talked, her blood, her flesh, all the people like her who had humiliated all the people like him. If he let go he would fall. It would almost be a relief. But anger kept him conscious.

Amanda went on cheerfully, "You'd still be alive when you hit those rocks. They'd go right up inside you. Once they found a fisherman down there. He was washed up in a storm. They kept wondering why he didn't go out with the tide. Then they saw he couldn't. Know why?"

He started to say the *Ave* again, this time in Latin to help him concentrate. He had learned that in parochial school. The nuns had taught him to say the *Ave* and the *Pater Noster* in Latin, and also the responses when he was an altar boy, before they changed the Mass. *Ave Maria, gratia plena—*

". . . and half his head had been beaten right in, and most of his face—"

He gave in. "All right. You can come to the cottage. Now go get help. Now."

"Promise?"

"Yeah. Promise. Go on."

It was too late, anyway. The huge blue sky swam in front of his face. *Pater noster, qui est in coeli . . .*

After a while his head cleared a little. He looked up toward the sky, now steady, but large and indifferent. The cliff was empty. She had gone. She had gone to get help, maybe. Maybe not. Probably not. He had given in for nothing. Desperately, he gave a final cry, "Help!"

"Catch it, stupid."

Something light fell against his body. He opened his eyes and saw a narrow rope lying over him. Gingerly he moved his arm and grasped it. It gave him a ridiculous sense of security, something reaching him from above, touching him.

Then there was a tug and the rope twitched out of his hand. He gave a cry.

Amanda peered over the edge. "I said hold it. I'm just pulling it around the rock to make it tight so you can hang onto it. Here." The end flapped toward him again, and, resenting her more than ever, he folded his hand around it and held on. Just wait until he got out of this. He'd teach her a thing or two. She had him now, but as soon as he got out he'd show her.

"Idiot," she said finally, and disappeared again.

Amanda ran up the steps, across the porch and pulled open the front door, letting it slam behind her.

"That boy from the cottage has fallen over the cliff," she announced to Miss Cathaway, who was writing a letter at the desk in the corner of the living room.

"Wolf, wolf!" Miss Cathaway said, not looking up.

Amanda frowned. "It's for real. You'd better call the police. They have ropes and things for rescuing people."

"After that business about the bath, Amanda, I'm leery of your fondness for practical jokes. No sale!"

Amanda lifted the lid off a glass jar on the hall table and took out a large piece of rock candy which she put whole into her mouth. From the latter emerged a mumble.

"What did you say?" the governess asked pointedly.

Amanda shifted the candy a little and wiped her mouth on the sleeve of her jersey. "I said, he's probably dead by now, anyway. He looked pretty putrid when I left him and that was at least fifteen minutes ago. But if you don't care, why should I?" She gave an elaborate shrug. "But don't blame me if his mangled body's found under the cliff. Did I tell you about that fisherman who—"

"Yes," Miss Cathaway said hurriedly. "I'm writing a letter, Amanda. We'll play games later."

"You'll be sorry."

"Why don't you call the police, then?"

It was a telling dig. More than once Amanda had routed out the Island's entire rescuing and fire-fighting equipment for a wholly fictitious crisis.

Amanda stamped her foot. "This is for real. He's caught in that laurel tree that sticks out under the Point. Don't just sit there. The tree's about to crack. I threw him that rope from the garage, but it's only for him to hang onto. If he falls it'll never hold him."

For a second, consternation showed on the governess's face. Then she visibly braced herself. "And pigs might fly. I don't believe you, Amanda. You love nothing better than for me to look foolish—"

Mrs. Little's large bulk came through the baize door connecting the front of the house with the kitchen. "Is that someone on the beach calling? Or am I imagining it? I heard it when I was coming in from the wash house, and then again when I was hanging out—" She broke off and stared at the governess's white face, "What in heaven's the matter?"

Miss Cathaway gave a gasp, sprang up, and ran across the room to the old-fashioned telephone.

"Police—police! Oh, operator! Please hurry!"

Amanda elaborately licked her fingers. "I told her that boy from the cottage was hanging practically by a hand from the tree on the cliff. But she *wouldn't* believe me. Maybe the next time—that is, if he's alive—"

Miss Cathaway cried, "Oh, do be quiet, Amanda! Is that the police? That boy from the cottage has fallen over the cliff below the Point and is hanging in the tree. Amanda told me. No, not this time. She's telling the truth. Mrs. Little heard him, too. All right. I'll meet you there. And I'll call the doctor."

"Of course, if he's dead, you'll have to explain to his family how come help wasn't gotten to him in time," Amanda said, lounging against the door. "Even if they don't put you in prison for neglecting your duty, it will haunt you for the rest—"

"Amanda," Miss Cathaway's voice had risen. Frantically she was rattling the arm of the telephone to get the operator again. "If you don't be quiet this instant, I'll come over and slap you. I mean it. Operator, please get me Dr. Townsend right away. He might be in the hospital now."

"And if she doesn't," Mrs. Little eyed Amanda who was slouching over to the desk to see what Miss Cathaway had written, "I will. Oh, no, you don't." She moved quickly and slammed the desk top up before Amanda got to it.

Amanda danced away. "First you have to catch me." When she got to the front door she turned and put out her tongue, made a Bronx cheer, and fled outside.

"You've broken your ankle and bruised your head. That's why you kept going in and out. Other than that you're okay. But don't go wandering around the Island in one of our fogs or you'll be in worse trouble. Not until you know it better."

The doctor adjusted the bandage and poked at the cast on Malcolm's foot. "That seems to be pretty firm. Sure you want to go back to the cottage? We can keep you here a couple of days and you'd get taken care of—meals and all that."

"No, thanks. I'd rather get back to the cottage."

He had a funny feeling about the cottage. If he didn't get back who knew what Amanda might be doing among his things.

"All right. I'll drive you."

The doctor stared down at the boy with the thin face and angry eyes. He wasn't really hurt badly enough to insist on holding him in the tiny Island hospital, although he could truss the boy up so that he would have to stay and they could keep an eye on him. But it would be a little like caging a wild animal.

Malcolm was already on his feet, or rather his one foot, propped on the crutches the nurse had dug out from somewhere.

The doctor eyed them doubtfully. "You may find it hard getting around on those, harder than you think."

"I've used 'em before," Malcolm said briefly. "I'll be okay."

"How about food?"

"Maybe they'll deliver from the store."

"Yes. When Gil's son, Mike, is around. But in summer he's mostly out on the boats, like most of the kids around here, those that don't go onto the Mainland. I'll bring you some stuff this afternoon, if Mike isn't there. After that, you'll have to make up an order twice a week for the delivery truck that drives in from the Mainland."

"What do people up at the Big House do?"

"They get deliveries from the truck, but if they need something in the meantime, Mrs. Little drives down to the village in her car, or sends the gardener in his."

"They all have cars?"

"You pretty well have to on this Island. Otherwise you'd be trapped in."

Malcolm's dark eyes shifted restlessly to the window and the manicured lawn outside the hospital. "Any time you want to leave," the doctor said on impulse, "I'll drive you to the airport or to the bus station on the Mainland."

"Why should I want to leave?"

"No reason. It was just an offer. If you're ready I'll drive you to the cottage." He could almost feel the boy's resentment.

"I take it Amanda discovered you over the cliff?" the doctor said, easing his car through the hospital gates. They were on the southern part of the Island, the other side of the village.

"Yeah." The memory of the promise that had been forced out of him infuriated him. He'd make her pay.

The doctor went on, "It was good she did, and that for once she behaved like a decent human being and went to get help."

Malcolm said nothing. He wasn't about to admit the blackmail he'd had to submit to.

Noting the silence and the scowl, the doctor wondered what had actually gone on. "She's an odd child," he said.

"You can say that again!" The words burst out of Malcolm before he could stop himself.

The doctor glanced at him. "Does she bother you?"

"Na." A sort of angry curiosity prodded him. "Is she nuts or something? She seems to think the cottage belongs to her. When I tell her to scat she blows her top."

"Yes—no . . . I don't know. She certainly needs something but I'm not sure what it is. Miss Cathaway—her governess—tells me that her father has threatened to send her to some kind of school for disturbed children."

"A nut school, huh! That'd teach her."

"It would indeed," the doctor said drily.

They rode up on the single paved road bordering stretches of green pasture. The chill, sweet air, smelling of salt and pine, came through the open windows. The sky was a cloudless blue. Malcolm remembered what it looked

like when he lay like a spread-eagled bug on its back in the
tree, and shivered.

"Cold?" the doctor asked kindly.

Malcolm started to shake his head, found it hurt and said,
"No. Where's her mother?" he asked abruptly.

"She died about four years ago."

"Tough."

The doctor would ordinarily have left it at that. But
something in the boy's tone made him add, "Yes. It was.
And when she was here she wasn't much of a mother—or,
for that matter, a wife." He added the last almost to himself.

"Yeah? How so?"

"She—Well, I guess you could say she liked a good time.
And not the kind of good time you get on the Island. Bright
lights and people and fashionable clothes and admiration.
All the things she had had before she married Amanda's
father. She was a taker, not a giver." He relapsed into
silence for a minute and then went on, "She was lonely and
probably felt cold-shouldered. I guess she was getting her
own back, with the flirtation and the dallying. The pity
of it is, I think Hamilton looks at Amanda and sees her
mother. It may sound crazy to you that a child like Amanda,
surrounded by servants and governesses and money should
be deprived. But in my better moments that is what I realize
she is."

"Poor little rich girl," Malcolm sneered.

"It depends, I suppose, on what you mean by rich."

Malcolm shifted his leg. "And in your not-so-kind
moments?"

"I want to take a brush to her."

They turned off the road and headed down the lane
toward the cottage. The doctor asked, "Will your ankle
interfere with your playing? Will your music suffer?"

"I don't play with my feet."

But he was afraid, nevertheless, that in some strange way it would.

Amanda arrived the next morning. To his fury she had obviously come through the window because she just marched downstairs and into the kitchen while he was having breakfast. "Boy, is this place a mess," she said, pushing the connecting door open.

It was. The doctor had emptied a few ashtrays but they were full again, and Malcolm had driven the doctor out before he'd had a chance to see the dirty dishes.

He leaned back in his chair. His foot, propped on a straight chair in front of him, was aching. He was eating off the kitchen table, sitting sideways. Dirty plates stood in piles on the drainboard and leaned drunkenly together in the sink. He'd always refused to wash dishes. "Woman's work," his father had said. And although he'd hated his father for a lot of things—not being there mostly—he agreed with him about this. After all, there were his mother and five giggling sisters. Why should he wash a dish?

He eased his foot. "Well—wash 'em up, then."

She stopped in front of him, elbows out, fists on her skinny hips. "Who do you think you are?"

He leaned forward. "I know who I am. I'm Malcolm Sanderson and I've got a busted ankle, but even if I didn't, I'm a man and I don't wash dishes—not unless I want to," he added prudently. Sooner or later he might have to, and he didn't want it to look as though he were backtracking. "I'll wash 'em when I get ready," he said, to make it quite clear.

"You'll get mice and cockroaches," she said, outraged.

He shrugged. "So? Big deal. Why should I care?"

Cleanliness had never impressed itself on Amanda as a

virtue to be admired and sought. But vermin crawling over *her* cottage because this slum lout didn't know enough to wash up was something else. "You're a pig! A filthy pig."

She saw him jerk forward and realized with pleasure that she could stand out of his reach and insult him as much as she wanted. "You're a—"

But despite her distance, the look on his face frightened her. "Listen, kid. I keep my promises. You can come here. I won't stop you. But if I have any of your lip I'll write your father. I'll tell him how you left me over that cliff while you took your time about getting help. I could be dead, you know, if that tree had cracked. I'll tell him how you're in and out of this house all the time, getting in my hair, against his orders, and how you won't even help me with a dish, even though I've busted my leg. I hear your old man's going to send you to some kind of a nut school if you give him any more trouble. So I'm telling you. You can come here because I said so, but if you give me any trouble I'm writing to your old man, and it's me he's going to believe, kid, not you. There are two sides to this bargain, and don't you forget it."

There was a brief silence. The clock on the wall ticked and struck ten o'clock. At the sound one of the old kitchen windows rolled down a little from the top. The sweet, tangy air blew in, bringing with it the sound of the gulls, wheeling over the cliff.

"Pooh," Amanda said in a high squeak. "You wouldn't dare." But she said it purely to keep her end up, not because she believed it, and they both knew it.

chapter five

Amanda made a point of dropping in each day, sometimes in the morning, sometimes in the afternoon, through the front door, the back door or the window. Twice when she walked in Malcolm was sitting on the piano stool, staring at the paper on the rack in front of him. Once he threw a book at her. "Scat!" he yelled. She put her tongue out and ran upstairs.

But more often, particularly as the days wore on, he would be slouched in the huge wing chair beside the empty fireplace, the ashtrays beside him full, and a pile of stubs in the hearth. Once when Amanda went out to the kitchen to help herself to whatever she could find to eat, she saw ants and some kind of bugs running over the dishes in the sink. There was an odd smell in the kitchen which she finally tracked down to the pantry, where there were five

separate piles of dirty dishes stacked on the stone floor, and
as she opened the door there was a scuttle of little feet. She
marched into the living room.

"What's the matter with you? This place *smells!*"

He stared straight at her. "So what? So do you. You
smell worse than my sisters and you don't live in a tenement, Miss Fancy Pants. How many bathrooms have you
got in that palace up there?"

"None of your business."

He leaned forward. The white around the black irises
was bloodshot, and there were smudgy discs under his eyes
as though he hadn't slept.

"Anything I want to know is my business."

"Sez you. You're nothing but a dirty slum boy. You
don't know how to live with decent people. My mother
always said—"

"Your mother was no good."

Amanda went red. "She was, too. Just who do you think
you are talking—"

"And your father can't even stand to think about her.
That's why he can't stand you. Everybody on the Island
knows—"

But the words were drowned out. Amanda, screeching
and flailing her fists, came at him. He caught the two hands
in one of his and held them, laughing. "You're no better
than the girls on the street in that slum I live in. Only
there's some reason for them. There's none for you. You're
just a high-class nut and they're going to put you in a
high-class nut house with high-class bars. But they're still
bars, and you can screech your tonsils out and they won't
even bother to listen. They'll just poke food at you through
the door, and send off reports to your father that you're
doing well, and he'll be so glad not to have to see you that

he'll be happy to pay the money not to come near the place."

She was sobbing now, and trying half-heartedly to aim a kick at his shin. But his arm was long as well as strong, and he held her off like a tiresome puppy.

She yelled, "It's not true. It's not true. He loves me. He loves me as much as Chuck or Giselle or Buzz. He does, he does."

"Yeah? Then why isn't he here? Why are you making so much noise?" But he was worried. Her face was a queer color, and there was a wild, unfocused look in her eyes. "C'mon," he said more gently. He didn't want accusations of harassing his benefactor's daughter to be leveled at him. Also, having vented on her his own frustrations—the terrible, mind-splitting kind that always gripped him when he couldn't work—he felt something akin to remorse. "Look, I didn't mean all of it. But you come around here bothering me and yelling at me, what d'you expect?"

He had her skinny little body in his hands now, his fingers around her narrow ribs. Her head was hunched down and she was heaving in spasms. A memory tore at him, a hot night when he was sleeping on the fire escape and woke to hear from the room inside the despairing sobs of his little sister, the one with the crooked back who had died a little while afterward. He had carefully kept his mind away from that, because of all his sisters, Florita had irritated him most for the simple reason that she had adored him. Whenever he was trying to study or compose or just think she would trot up beside him and poke at his arm or leg and, more often that not, he would push her away. And in some way, although her back wasn't crooked and her face wasn't as pretty as Florita's, this wretched Amanda made him think of her.

He shook her. "Be quiet!"

But the sobs had settled into a steady, desolate cry.

"C'mon, kid. It's not that bad. I'm sorry."

"Nobody loves me. Nobody cares what happens to me. Everybody wants me to go away. Father hates me, he hates me, he HATES me. He thinks I'm UGLY."

Madre de Dios, he thought. Life in high places was not as different as he imagined. "You're not so bad," he said. "Clean up a little, comb your hair, and you'll be okay. Pretty, even."

For the first time the drowned amber eyes looked up at him. "Do you think so?" Amanda whispered.

"Sure."

She rubbed her eyes. He released her. She went over to the hearth and pushed a few butts into the fireplace with her foot. For a while she stood with her back to him, rolling the butts back and forth with her sneaker. Then she drew a breath, groped around the pockets of her jeans, and finally wiped her nose on the sleeve of her jersey. "Got any detergent?" she asked.

"Why?" The mellow mood was going. His head was beginning to ache.

"Somebody's got to do the dishes."

For a moment he was tempted to tell her he'd do his own dishes when he got around to it. But the sight of his crutch, propped against the table, plus the ache in his foot, plus something approaching sympathy, born out of the doctor's words, stopped him. "There's some under the sink," he said.

A while after she left the room he heard the sound of water running and the unmistakable noise of a dish falling on the stone floor and breaking. Well, it wasn't his dish, or his mother's. If it had been and he or one of his sisters had dropped it, he could imagine his mother's voice scaling up, the words lashing out, and later, the slap. Dishes were expensive.

But what was a dish more or less to the rich? As though to underline his thought, there was another crash. Amanda, wet from her neck to her knees, appeared in the doorway.

"I busted a couple of your dishes."

"They're not mine. They're yours."

"That's right. I forgot. Well—" She shrugged and went back in.

After a while he pulled himself up and, using the backs of a couple of chairs, hopped over to the piano. Even before he sat down he could feel himself tighten. His fingers felt thick, like sausages, and there was nothing in his head—no sound, no rhythm. He stared at the staved sheets in front of him, only the top lines were filled. He played them, to get himself started, and then played them again, but his hands came to a stop.

"Stuck?" said Amanda, beside him.

He turned savagely, his hand out to whack her over the ear. But caution intruded. She was not his sister or one of the neighborhood children. She was Amanda Hamilton and her father was on the board of the Conservatory. One word from him, Malcolm thought, and he could get Malcolm thrown out. Resentment boiled up in him.

"Why don't you leave me alone. You've got this whole lousy estate to run around in. Why bother me?"

"You said I could come here."

"You can. But if you pester me I'll leave and when I go I'll do what I said—write to your father and tell him why."

She had that funny look again. Her mouth opened and a screech started to come out.

"What on earth—?" The doctor strode through the front door. "Amanda!" He put his bag down and went toward her. She stopped screeching and started to dodge away from him. Malcolm, watching, forgot his ill-humor and started to laugh.

She was outdodging the doctor easily, her agile little form darting around the chairs. Without thinking, Malcolm stuck out his foot—the one with the cast on it—and she tripped over it.

"Thank you," the doctor said, and nabbed her as she tried to pick herself up from the floor.

Malcolm frowned. He had stopped her without thinking. Heaven alone knew what she would say. "I was teasing her," he said.

"Well she shouldn't go into a spasm like this. It's not good for her. Her father—"

"I wasn't doing anything," Amanda said loudly. "I washed his stinking dishes."

"Washed the dishes?" The doctor sounded incredulous.

"Yeah. She did."

Surprise had made the doctor loosen his grip. Amanda twisted away. "We were just having an—an argument."

"You certainly were." The doctor felt angry and foolish. He had thought for a minute that the boy had lost his temper with her and struck, which would be understandable, but nevertheless, Amanda was a child and he had felt it his duty to interrupt and go after her. "What's going on?"

"Nothing. I told you. We were arguing." Amanda stared hostilely at him.

The doctor gave up. "Run on home, Amanda," he said, taking his bag over to the chair near Malcolm.

"No."

The doctor turned. "Do as I say," he said quietly.

"I don't have to obey you." She stood her ground. A sodden dish towel was wrapped around her middle. Soapy water was drying on her jersey, leaving high watermarks. Her black hair was a tangled mop. Defiantly, she was picking her nose.

Like a little jungle cat, Malcolm thought, or like one of the alley scavengers of the city, sending their lost yowls into the night, but spitting at the sound of a footstep, defending their wretched garbage against dogs, children, and drunks. How on earth did she come to be born into this plush setting among these people armored against the claws of life with their "please" and "thank you." He scowled at her. "Blow! Scat!"

A resounding Bronx cheer bubbled from her. She held her nose with her hand. "Pee-ew, stink you!" Then she lifted her hand, thumb first, against her nose in a universal gesture.

Malcolm grinned. "Same to you."

As she left, Amanda aimed a kick at his cast, missed, and fled through the door.

When the doctor had gone Malcolm tried once again, starting with the two lines of music already written, all he had succeeded in doing since he arrived three weeks before. He played them slowly, he played them fast, but when he came to the end, he stopped, unable to find the next step in the theme. In fury and frustration he pounded the piano, then put his elbows on the polished wood and his head in between. Above his head his fists clenched.

This was the way people went nuts, he thought, and wondered if that was what was happening to him. Quite suddenly he understood, for the first time, what made his mother suddenly lash out—physically and verbally—at the children. Always before, in great bitterness, he had blamed her, as he blamed his father for other things. But he knew now that if one of his sisters, or Amanda, were here, he would strike out at them to relieve the queer pounding in his head. To stop it, he straightened and, without conscious thought of what he was going to play, ran his hands over the keys. The music he had learned from his professor did not meet the moment's need—it was too disciplined, too much from the outside. Instead, he broke into some of the melodies and rhythms he had grown up with, his mother's records—marimbas, fiesta music, his mother called it—and others he had brought himself, the guitar in another mood, somber and evocative.

It satisfied his angry nerves as nothing else could have done. Into it he wove some rock and let it build until it swelled, part jungle, part Spanish, part folk-American. He played until he could smell the melting tar on the hot asphalt, a whiff of decaying garbage, the faint, sweet perfume his sisters and the girls he went out with wore, the hot tamales and chili. He heard the sounds: the shouts, the giggles of his neighborhood, alive, chattering and dancing on a hot summer night, a million miles away from this Anglo-Saxon paradise with its deaf ears and good manners and cold heart.

Outside hunched on the damp earth beneath his window, Amanda shivered with cold and a queer, racy delight. After a while, she tried the door, found it open, and crept in. Malcolm didn't even hear her as she crossed the room outside his line of vision. A northern setting sun crept in the window, but it was cold, and her jersey was still damp. Going out to the kitchen she closed the door silently, dug around till she found a pile of newspapers, crumpled up several sheets, and came back into the living room. Malcolm, lost somewhere on the hot streets of his boyhood, played on and didn't hear.

What with the butts, the rest of the dirty paper he had thrown into the fireplace, the crumpled-up balls she'd brought, and some kindling from one of the scuttles at the side, it was easy to start a fire and she sat down with her back to the stone wall next to it. After a while she got up, went out, got some milk and bread, came back, put on some logs, and sat down again.

Malcolm played on. His hair was tousled. His mouth lost its thinness and relaxed into softer, more boyish curves. He looked younger, more like sixteen or seventeen than nineteen. Amanda, her knees crossed, replete with milk and buttered bread, dozed.

After a while he stopped playing and rested, his hands on his knees. Amanda opened her eyes. For the first time Malcolm seemed to notice the fire. "That's nice," he said, forgetting to sound tough.

Uncrossing her knees, Amanda stood up, hesitated, then went over to the piano. Since he was sitting, Malcolm's head was just about on a level with hers. For a moment they looked at each other. Then, without a thought beforehand of what she was going to do, Amanda leaned forward and put her arms around his neck. Startled into a response, he put his around her thin little body. She snuggled against his side, propped her chin on his shoulder, and gave a sigh of contentment.

Malcolm, astonished at himself as much as at Amanda, said nothing for a moment. Part of him wanted to whack her away, part of him was inclined to be gentle.

After a while he compromised and muttered awkwardly, "All right, kid. C'mon. I'm not your old man." He gave a vague pat to the shoulder blade that stuck out like a coat hanger under his hand.

"Too true," said Amanda, stepping back and wiping her nose on the sleeve of her jersey.

Malcolm watched her. "I thought you were supposed to

be the ritzy kind. You're no better than my sister. Don't
you have a handkerchief or something?"

"No. I never have one. Handkerchiefs are a drag and
always getting lost. What is your sister like?"

"Which one?" He grinned. "I've got five."

"Gee." When she was least self-conscious she used the
milder expletives. He suspected that she used the others
deliberately, with malice aforethought, to shock.

"The one you said I'm no better than."

"Florita," he said.

Amanda clasped her fingers around his arm. "Is she nice?
Do you like her?"

He pulled himself up, but remained looking down at
her. "She was a pest, like you."

"But do you like her?"

"Sometimes I did. She's dead."

"Oh. Well then, maybe I can be Florita. Can I?"

"No." He saw her flinch and added, "You don't want
to be somebody else, somebody dead."

"I do, too. If you liked her."

"Look. Stop pestering me."

She dropped her hand but didn't move.

"I said you're okay." He flicked her cheek and cuffed
her gently on the head. A brilliant smile radiated her face.
"Tell me about Florita. Please. And your family. And
where you live. I liked that music a lot. Much better than
the other. Please tell me. Will you?" She was jumping up
and down.

"Quiet down. That's just trash. It's not good. Street
music."

"But will you tell me, please? You know about me. Tell
me about your sisters and where you live?"

Curiously, he was tempted. The music had pulled some

old strings in him. He was homesick. "Okay. Let me get a Coke or something." Using one crutch, he hobbled out to the kitchen and came back carrying a bottle.

They sat down, backs to the sofa, in front of the fire, and he told her about his street, his sisters and mother, about the chili and *frijoles* and the marimbas, and even a little about the gangs and the fights which she liked best of all. When he paused, she said, "That's what your music's like."

He frowned. "But I don't want it to be like that. I want it to be good."

"I liked it," she said stubbornly, and then put her fingers in her ears as Miss Cathaway's voice came screeching down from the Big House.

"Better go," Malcolm said. "Or she'll be down here."

Amanda weighed the dangers and possibilities. "I suppose so."

Sighing, she got to her feet. Going to the window she screamed, "Coming!" And added under her breath, "You old witch." Then she put one hand on the windowsill and vaulted through. She stuck her head back in. "Good-bye." Then she ran up the long slope leading to the Big House.

chapter six

"It isn't that she is any better," Miss Cathaway said unhappily a week or so later. "It just seems that way because she's almost never here. I only see her at breakfast and supper and occasionally—if I shout myself hoarse—lunch."

She and Mrs. Little were finishing breakfast at the kitchen table. Amanda had not yet come downstairs. Mrs. Little put her plate, cup, saucer, and orange-juice glass in a neat pile and pushed herself up. "Spends her time down at the cottage with that hoodlum," she said. "Just like her father told her not to. Lord knows what she'll pick up." She carried the dishes over to the sink and started running water over them.

"Bad language for one thing," Miss Cathaway said gloomily.

Mrs. Little turned off the tap and dried her hands. "Thought she knew all the words."

"Well, she produced a new one this morning. At least I've never heard her use it."

"She needs the back of a hairbrush."

"She needs someone she can have affection and respect for," Miss Cathaway said with surprising firmness.

Mrs. Little moved toward her own staircase, leading to her room. "You've been reading too many of those books. You've got yourself all muddled with a lot of those high-sounding theories, like that hoity-toity nurse that was here. 'Permissive' this and 'rejection' that. Tcha." She passed out of sight, leaving Miss Cathaway feeling rather crushed.

Amanda clattered in through the dining-room door and sat down. The governess, waiting hopefully for some acknowledgment of her existence, watched silently as Amanda drank down all her orange juice and half her milk and helped herself to a buttered English muffin. Obviously Amanda was not about to observe the amenities, so Miss Cathaway cleared her throat and said dutifully, but without much hope, "Please tidy your room before you go out, Amanda."

"Why should I?" Amanda said experimentally. She was trying to see how far Mousy Cathy could be pushed.

Miss Cathaway looked at her speculatively. "Just for the novelty of doing something that somebody asks, perhaps."

Amanda didn't deign a reply. Her breakfast finished, she got up from the table, put a large piece of bubble gum in her mouth and loped out to the front of the house. Without looking where she was going she plunged down the porch steps and all but ran into a state trooper.

"Whoa there," he said in a friendly fashion. "Where's the fire?"

Amanda looked with admiration at his uniform, the polished black boots and belt, the helmet, and most of all the holster. His motorcycle, black and aggressive-looking, was parked on the gravel. She sauntered toward it. "Are you going to arrest Old Cathy?" she said, raising her voice hopefully in case anyone might be listening and swinging a jaunty leg over the saddle.

The state trooper strolled over to where Amanda, rising up and down, was making throttlelike noises in her throat and fiddling with the controls. Thoughtfully he bent over her and withdrew the ignition key.

"Whatcha think I was going to do?" Amanda asked in her Humphrey Bogart voice. "Steal it?"

The blue eyes crinkled. "Would you?"

Amanda shrugged elaborately. "Why not? Put the key back and see."

"I might want to make a fast getaway."

"Oh, funny man. You kill me." Holding her stomach she rolled around the saddle.

"Yeah? Well try this on for laughs. Who's in your guest cottage?"

Amanda sat up and casually blew out her bubble gum. "Wouldn't you like to know?"

"Not really. But if I get two answers to three questions I'll win a box of Cracker Jack."

"Man, you crack me up!" Amanda played for time. "What are the other two?"

"How come you're so smart is one of them?" the trooper said good-naturedly.

"Born that way, I guess." Amanda threw her gum down meaning to miss his boot by an inch. Unfortunately, it hit, sticking to his instep.

"That'll teach me," he said, and bending down, neatly picked it off. He stood there, holding it delicately between his fingers. His freckled, intelligent face smiled. Amanda braced herself for the worst.

"Now let's see," he said pleasantly. Amanda moved, but

not quickly enough. A large firm hand held her shoulder.

"Take your hand off me," she screamed.

A head stuck out of the first-floor hall window. "What's that?" Mrs. Little said.

"Police brutality," Amanda shrieked.

"Glory alleluia! Go to it, Sergeant. Need any help?"

The sergeant grinned. "I don't think so. I'm just figuring out the best place—artistically speaking—to put the gum she so kindly threw on my foot."

"How about down her throat?" Mrs. Little said, above the noise Amanda was making.

Miss Cathaway ran out of the house. "Amanda!—Oh," she finished, seeing the trooper. A strapping young man, he was easily holding Amanda while she squirmed and thrashed. "What did she do?" Miss Cathaway asked, crushing a desire to turn around and leave Amanda to it. The young man looked so entirely able to take care of the situation.

"Threw her gum at me."

"Police brutality," Amanda squeaked, but with less conviction.

"If he gave you a thorough spanking you'd deserve it," Miss Cathaway said.

The trooper's eyes twinkled. "Shall I?"

Against every impulse Miss Cathaway shook her head. The trooper released his hold.

"Sadist," Amanda said. She remembered his question. "What was that you said about the cottage?" Her lynx eyes watched him from under her brows.

"I said, who's there?"

Amanda glanced up quickly at the house. Mrs. Little's head was no longer visible. Old Cathy, of course, was hanging around where she wasn't wanted. She did some quick thinking. "There's the phone again," she said loudly.

"What phone?" Miss Cathaway looked around in a puzzled way.

Amanda shrugged. "Maybe I was wrong. I thought it was the long-distance operator again."

"What do you mean 'again,' Amanda? No long-distance operator called this morning."

"You were in the bathroom. I forgot to tell you. Operator four nine in New York wanted you to call back as soon as possible."

Miss Cathaway, her innocent soul the victim of too many such ploys, looked doubtful. "Amanda, are you telling the truth?"

Amanda shrugged. "Suit yourself. There was a man at the other end and he sounded mad."

"Probably wanted you," the trooper said.

Amanda glared at him. "It was *about* me," she said. "I'm pretty sure of that. But the operator wouldn't let me take it," she said virtuously.

"I'd better see." Despite all her doubts, Miss Cathaway knew she would have to go and investigate. She couldn't forget the episode of the cliff.

"Actually," Amanda said, as the governess disappeared behind the front door, "it's a great secret. Who's in the cottage, I mean."

"But you'll share it with me, won't you?" the trooper said engagingly.

Amanda mentally put him on the rack and started turning the handle. *Crunch. Bones breaking. Groans. He'd plead with her, sobbing for his wife and children. More slowly, Torturor, please.* "Are you married?" Amanda asked, momentarily diverted by her fantasy.

"Yes. I have a wife in every town. It's only fair, I feel, to the female populace. Would you like to be put on my waiting list?"

*After he fainted he was revived, and his broken body low-
ered into the bubbling oil.* "About the cottage," Amanda
said loudly. "Actually, it's a writer friend of my father's."

"Oh? Which one?"

"He's incognito."

"Old Iggy. How's his book coming?"

Amanda hated him. "I'm telling you the truth."

"All tuckered out, eh. No new stories?"

Amanda glared at him. "Well, who do *you* think it is?"

"How does Manuel Santiago grab you?"

"Never heard of him." But she felt curiously cold.

"No? Sometimes goes under the name of Malcolm
Sanderson."

She shrugged. "Could go under a lot of names, but I
don't think it's him."

"You don't? Then there's no use in even looking, is
there?"

"This one's about sixty-three, gray mustache, bald head,
fat stomach," Amanda improvised.

"Rock Hudson, eh? Didn't know he took up writing."
The trooper was walking up to the house.

"You're wasting your time," Amanda yelled after him.
Then she turned and ran swiftly down to the cottage.

As she neared the cottage she heard something new—
the sound of a guitar. The music gave her a strange feeling,
sad and wild.

"What's that?" she said, walking in.

"Flamenco."

"What's flamingo?"

Malcolm looked up and grinned. "Not flamingo, you
dope." His fingers plucked the strings. "Flamenco."

She went up and stood beside him. "What is it?"

"Spanish music. Gypsy music."

"Are you Gypsy?"

"My father's mother was part Gypsy."

"Are you a Spic?"

He moved so fast, Amanda didn't know what had happened until she found herself being shaken back and forward as though she had no spine at all. She tried to yell, but she couldn't get her breath. Beating against his arm did no good, but after a while he stopped and flung her across the room. She landed on the sofa.

"Don't you ever call me that again," Malcolm said. "Or I'll beat your brains out." Rage and pain tore at her, but she lay there, her face in the cushions fighting it, because she knew that she had no power over him. Between the two of them, power went the other way and she was helpless. Pride kept her face in the pillow. He must not see her cry.

There was a silence. She strained to hold her shoulders rigid. After a while he groped around for the crutch and limped over. "All right," he said, standing over her. "Get up. You're not dead."

Quickly she scrambled up, keeping her back to him, and tried to get over the back of the sofa. But he caught her by the back of her shirt. "Let go," she said fiercely.

Somehow he managed to turn her around. The grubby, streaked face stared back at him.

"Why did you call me a Spic?"

"I didn't. I asked you what a Spic was?"

"But you were just doing it to make me sore. You know what a Spic is. Spanish. Spanish-American."

"So?"

"So don't ever use it again, you lousy little gringo. It's an insult, and I don't take insult from you or any other *Norte Americano*."

She twisted free. "You keep your stinking hands to yourself, you SPIC!"

He slapped her, good and hard, right across the face, caught her with his crutch hand by the back of the shirt and raised his other hand again. "You say that again and this time you'll get it on the mouth. It won't feel so good. And you won't look so good without your front teeth."

"You wouldn't dare. My father'd kill you. He'd have you put in jail."

"Yeah? Okay. So I'd be in jail. Then he'd have to go and buy you some false teeth. How'd you like that?"

"Is it a private fight, or can anyone join in?" said a voice from the doorway.

Malcolm let go and straightened. His face had turned a dirty white. He looked as though all his life he had looked up to see a policeman watching him.

The trooper came in, his chestnut head almost reaching the ceiling. "You all right, kid?"

"Sure." Slowly, so she wouldn't show how shaky she was, she got down from the sofa and strolled toward the door. "He's teaching me karate," she said and blew out her new piece of bubble gum. "Only he gets sore when I practice it on him, now with his leg and everything."

The trooper frowned. He hadn't seen too much of what had happened. He glanced at the boy. "Is that true?"

Malcolm swallowed. Amanda loitered near the door, hopping around on one foot, examining the sole of the other. The trooper had the distinct impression that the young hood was going through some inner struggle. "Yeah," Malcolm finally said. "She's gettin' too good."

"You Malcolm Sanderson?"

"Yeah."

"Otherwise known as Manuel Santiago?"

"So what? I compose under a pseudonym."

The trooper said drily, watching him, "Some people would call it an alias."

"Yeah? Well, I wouldn't."

The trooper turned toward Amanda. "Run along home, Mata Hari. Your cobra milk will be waiting." The kid looked woebegone, he thought. "If you're at the motorbike when I get back there I'll give you a ride."

"Keep your stupid old ride, I'm busy." Head up, arms swinging like Colonel Bogey marching over the River Kwai, she strode up toward the Big House, determined not to wipe her cheeks or sniff until she was out of sound or sight.

chapter seven

Amanda didn't go near the cottage for four days, most of which she spent in her room staring moodily out the window. When driven out by Miss Cathaway's worried questions and tiresome suggestions, she climbed, surefooted as a mountain goat, down the cliff to the beach and sat broodingly on a rock, staring at the ocean and occasionally throwing stones.

On the fifth morning she took most of her books out of the shelves and flipped through them. "Garbage," she said, looking at one, and threw it on the floor.

At the end of an hour about twenty were lying about. But there were no clothes visible. Miss Cathaway had put them away.

She sat on the window seat, her ams around her knees, hugging them to her chest, her head resting on them. Through the trees to the left she could see the roof of the cottage and bits of white below. She wondered what Malcolm was doing. Not playing the piano, because with the window open she could hear him if he were. Possibly the guitar, though she could probably hear that, too. She imagined him sitting in the wing chair beside the fireplace, a scowl on his face, his crutch lying on the floor beside him. She wanted to go there so badly she could see herself shinny down the tree, across the lawn, over the fence, down through the field and the trees, and into the door of the cottage. But she didn't move.

"Nothing to do?" Miss Cathaway said brightly, standing in the doorway.

"Why don't you go off somewhere and die," Amanda said. She unwound her legs and stood up. Her fingers curled in her palm. "Nobody wants you. You're old and ugly and icky."

The governess had known the moment she spoke that she was being bright and irritating out of nervous habit. She clasped her hands in front of her, trying to still their trembling. "You certainly have an instinct for the jugular, Amanda. You know where to sink the knife." She paused. "That may be useful later in your life. But I don't think it will make you happy." Miss Cathaway turned and crossed the hall into her room, closing the door. Amanda scowled after her.

The front doorbell rang. Amanda tore down, beating Mrs. Little who was emerging slowly from the kitchen. She flung the door open. "Oh, it's you," she said to the doctor.

"Who were you expecting?" he said, coming in and putting his hat on the hall table.

"What's it to you?"

The child looked peaked, he thought, paying no attention to what she said. "Feeling all right?"

"I was, until you arrived."

"I can see you're in your usual good spirits." He went toward the kitchen and Mrs. Little's carbuncle. "Where is Miss Cathaway?"

"Sobbing her heart out in her room." She blew a bubble. It burst with a pink splat. "She says I have an instinct for the jugular."

"She's a perceptive woman, although even a crocodile would know that. I'm sorry it's been her lot to know you."

Amanda put her hand on the doorknob and blew her lips out in a Bronx cheer. It made a gratifying noise. Then she stuck out her tongue.

"Tell me," the doctor said. "Do you *like* people to hate you? You must, I suppose, because you work at it so hard. Even that young man down at the cottage was saying—"

Amanda went white. "You're lying!"

The doctor succumbed to an unexpected desire to avenge Miss Cathaway. "How do you know whether I am lying or not, since I haven't told you what Malcolm said?"

"I wouldn't believe anything you said, anyway," Amanda said, and to his astonishment, burst into tears. Pulling open the door, she ran across the veranda and down the steps.

The doctor was sorry almost immediately. She was, after all, a child. "Amanda—"

But she had gone.

As she neared the cottage she heard him playing. He must have started since she left her perch by the window. It wasn't what Amanda called his "composing" music. It was the music she liked much better, gypsy music. What was that funny word? Flamenco. But she could tell by the way he played that he was making it up as he went along, his fingers moving slowly, as though he were copying something in his head, groping along as it came clear. She sat down behind one of the trees at first, lashing her pride to keep her from going nearer. He had hit her. Had called her "gringo," which she knew from the stories he had regaled her with was an insult. Like *Norte Americano*. She didn't want to be a gringo or a *Norte Americano*. She wanted to be like him, and had practiced speaking with a Spanishy sort of accent when she was in the bath with the water running or in bed after Old Cathy had gone downstairs.

She was a Hamilton and he had hit her. But the magic of those thoughts seemed to have lost their power. Almost without her volition, she got up and moved slowly toward the cottage, shuffling her feet in the loose pine needles as she walked.

When she got to the window she sat down, so that the top of her head barely reached the sill. The music went on, bitter and haunting, but shot through with sweet every now and then. It made her want to dance. She got up and moved around, pushed by the beats. Then it stopped, so abruptly she was caught, one foot in front of another, her hip out, her arms up. She stood, frozen in this position.

"Hi," Malcolm said. His cast was gone. She saw a bandage beneath the bottom of his jeans. He stood in the door, his thumbs stuck in the top of his trousers.

She kicked some needles. "Hi."

"Where've you been?"

"Around."

A silence fell.

He shifted a little. "I'm sorry, kid. I shouldn't have belted you. But don't ever call a Spaniard a Spic. You'll get worse than I gave you."

She blinked hard. "I didn't know." Apologies came hard to her. "I'm sorry. Malcolm. Truly."

He grinned. "It's okay." He held out his hand. "Friends?"

She ran toward him.

It was more than he had bargained for, this funny kid clasping him around the neck, sobbing into his T-shirt. Florita came again to his mind. Awkwardly he put his arms around her. With one hand he patted her on the back. "Okay now. Take it easy. For crying out loud, Amanda, you're getting me wet."

Gently he lowered her to the ground. She wiped her nose on the sleeve of her jersey.

"The rich have sure been a disappointment to me," he said, handing her a crumpled handkerchief.

"When you leave can I go with you?" Amanda asked, blowing her nose.

"Go where?"

"Home. To your home."

"Are you nuts? Of course not."

"I wouldn't take up any room and I don't eat much. Everybody's always telling me I should eat more. I could go to school with your sisters."

He made a sound between a snort and a laugh. "Too much! You're too much! You've got so much money your father sends people like me to school and college. He gives money to the Conservatory. My family's whole apartment isn't as big as his office on Wall Street. My sisters—any girl I know—would give anything, and I mean *anything* at all, to live in a big house like that one up there with servants and cars and a chauffeur and a gardener. I bet you have a bathroom for every room, don't you?" He suddenly sounded more Spanish.

"What have bathrooms got to do with it?"

He looked down at her. "You know what my family had when I was little? A sink in the kitchen. That's all. That's it. We have a better apartment now. But once, not too long ago, it was like that. And people like you say

people like me don't bathe. You wouldn't bathe either if
you lived like that. My mother, when she isn't cooking is
washing, washing all the time—clothes, sheets, towels,
clothes again, every day, all the time so we'll be clean.
You've got a bathroom all your own and half the time
you're dirtier than my sisters."

"It's just that everybody keeps nagging me to take a
bath."

He grinned. "You mean the Establishment."

The tawny eyes sparkled. She gave a little whoop and
a skip. "Check. Zero-on. The Establishment!"

"Okay, okay. Cool it. I guess it's just like Mom says.
When you've got it, you don't appreciate it."

"Would you like me better if I took a bath every day?"

He shrugged. "It's nothing to me." The sparkle went
from her face. "Why should you care?" he asked.

Her face went pink. "Because I love you," she said
passionately.

He flushed. "You're a funny kid." He heard again the
voice of his little sister, *Hernando mio, yo te quiero mucho.*
Something made him add, "You ought to be careful who
you say that to."

"I've never said it to anybody—except . . ."

"Except who?"

"Father, once. And Bridie, once. Not that it matters,"
she said suddenly putting on The Hamilton Manner.

He grinned. "La-di-da."

She glared at him.

"Who was Bridie? What do you mean, it doesn't matter?"

"A governess."

"What happened to her? What did you do, poison her?"

"I hate you, hate you hate you HATE you," Amanda
screamed, rushing at him.

He stopped her easily with one arm. "So hate. Who

cares?" She thrashed helplessly. "Okay, Amanda, cut it out. Man, if you lived with us you'd get belted so hard you'd have nothing left to scream with. You're a rotten spoiled rich kid. You're not good enough to live with us." Indifferently, he turned his back and walked into the cottage.

Limping over to the chair he picked up his guitar and plucked at the strings. But he couldn't get Amanda's face, twisted with anger and pain, out of his head. "Spoiled rich kid," he muttered to himself, beneath the beat of the music. But it didn't quite do the trick. He was about to get up and see what she was up to when she came in. She was never pretty. But sometimes she looked interesting, her eyes blazing, her face alight. Right now she looked like a sodden stray kitten. Her cheeks were streaked. Her mouth drooped.

His heart gave a funny tug. "*Pobrecita*," he said, and smiled. He tightened a string.

She gave a slight hiccough, and walked over to him slowly. "I don't really hate you."

"Love, hate. It's often the same."

"Yes." She sat down cross-legged beside his chair and picked at the rug. "Can't I come home with you?"

"Your father wouldn't let you even drive through our street, let alone live with us." He tried to imagine Amanda with his sisters. Curiously, when he put his mind to it, it wasn't as outlandish a picture as it should be. She had the toughness necessary to stay alive in his neighborhood. But even so—his mind veered to other things. No. It was unthinkable.

"Father wouldn't have to know. And if it's the way you said he'd never look."

"No. Now stop pestering me. Besides. You shouldn't worry him like that."

"He wouldn't be that worried. He wants to send me

away, anyway, to That School. He'd make a lot of noise for a while. Then he'd forget."

He tried to imagine his mother—or even his father when he was home—"forgetting" about one of their children. Screams, yes. Beatings, yes. Fights, yes. Forgetting, no. For a second his mother's kitchen was around him, with its hot smells and tumbling voices and he had a sudden, overwhelming desire to be there, with his own family, to hear them and touch them. His own people. His hands played across the strings. With an effort he brought his mind back to Amanda. "Doesn't your father love you?"

"No. Does yours love you?"

"Of course. But he's away a lot."

"Why is he away a lot?"

He shrugged. "We are from Cuba. He works with other Cubans who are in Florida and other places."

"You mean like James Bond?"

"No. Not like James Bond. Like a poor Cuban who has no money, no land, no job, and here no profession." Angrily he struck the strings.

"Don't you care? About Cuba, I mean?"

"I hardly remember it. I am an American. Besides. There's my music."

"Wouldn't you like to be a revolutionary?"

He grinned. "Counterrevolutionary."

"Well, whatever it is. Don't you want to help him?"

"I told you. I must work at my music." He sounded angry. "Anyway, my father wants me to stay at the Conservatory."

Amanda sighed. "He sounds nice. Like he's for real."

"Yeah. When he's there. The rest of the time, while he is off fighting a hopeless battle that we will never win, Mother works, works, works to keep us clean and off the streets. You ask too many questions."

"Father's going to send me to That School," she said despairingly.

"Maybe you'll like it."

"No. I'll hate it."

He shrugged. "Then why not behave yourself?"

She stared at him angrily. "Why don't you? Why do you get into fights and smoke pot and—"

He leaned forward and grabbed her by the front of her jersey. "Did you tell anybody that? The governess? The doctor?"

"Of course not."

He let her go and leaned back. "Well somebody opened his big trap. That state trooper wanted to know if I had any up here. The cops at home had called."

"Do you?"

"No."

"I wouldn't tell," she said indignantly. "You *know* I wouldn't."

"Maybe. All dames talk."

"That's not true. I'm not a 'dame.' I wouldn't tell on you. You shouldn't say that." She had got up and was standing in front of him.

"Say what?" The state trooper, taking off his helmet was stepping through the doorway.

Amanda turned and stood, her feet apart. "Why don't you leave Malcolm alone?"

Malcolm lowered the guitar. His black eyes were hostile and a little afraid. "Yeah. Why don't you get off my back?"

The trooper put his helmet down. His eyes didn't twinkle so much today. "Run along, kid. Your father wouldn't want you to be here."

"Why not? How do you know?"

"Because I'm smart. Now are you going, or do I carry you up to the house?"

"You're a fink. A rat-fink."

The trooper was coming toward her. "How did you know?"

Malcolm got up. "Beat it, Amanda. Blow."

But he was too late. The trooper grabbed her as she passed. "I think," he said pleasantly, as she struggled and thrashed in his grip, "that I'm going to restore you to your loved ones."

"Malcolm!" she shrieked.

But the trooper bore her off under one arm. "Now," he said, as they got to his motorcycle, "you're going to get that ride you've been hankering for."

"I don't want your stinking ride. PUT ME DOWN!"

He plunked her down on the front of the saddle and swung on behind, one arm clamped around her middle. When she started to kick, he got her feet pinioned under his legs. "Comfortable?" he inquired solicitously.

"You big ape. You'll pay for this. I'll tell my father you—" But the rest was lost as he revved up the engine and roared toward the house.

Despite her fury Amanda loved the ride. She wondered if there were any lady troopers and if they had motorbikes of their own. . . .

"Wow!" she yelled, as they roared up the drive and stopped in a spray of gravel.

"How was that?" the trooper asked, dismounting.

Amanda remembered that he was The Enemy. She put on The Hamilton Manner. "A bore. A drag." Languidly she put her leg over the saddle and then made a spring for freedom.

"Oh, no!" the trooper said, putting out his foot.

Amanda went headlong. She spat out some grass. "Help! Police brutality!"

Miss Cathaway came running out of the house. Behind her was the doctor.

"He raped me!" Amanda shrieked.

"Amanda!" Miss Cathaway, halfway down the veranda steps, looked shocked.

The trooper seemed unmoved. "Passion overcame me," he explained, getting a firm grip on Amanda and lugging her toward the house.

The doctor grinned. "Serve her right."

"She shouldn't say things like that," Miss Cathaway protested stepping aside to let the trooper and Amanda pass.

"How are you going to stop her?" the doctor inquired. "She reads comics, paperbacks, and watches television. There are no mysteries to the young any more, good or bad."

"She shouldn't even *know* about such things at her age."

"What are you going to do?"

"What *can* one do?"

The trooper thrust Amanda through the front door, closed it, and stood, holding the knob. "Try and keep her inside for a while, will you. I have to talk to that kid down at the cottage, and I don't want her hanging around."

"Trouble?" the doctor said.

The trooper's pleasant face looked worried. "I'm not sure. Could be." He glanced toward Miss Cathaway. "Can you hold her here for a bit?"

"No," Miss Cathaway said. "I can't. If I lock her in her room she'll climb out the window and onto the veranda roof from which she can shinny down easily. If I lock the window I wouldn't put it past her to break the glass. There isn't a room she couldn't get out of."

"I see. Well, do the best you can. Maybe you can just distract her for a bit."

"A little like trying to distract a charging bull elephant,

but I'll help," the doctor said, taking his place at the front door.

The trooper grinned. "She's not a bad kid. Just needs handling."

"I don't suppose you'd care to adopt her," the doctor asked, as the trooper got on his motorcycle.

The trooper's smile broadened. "I wouldn't mind. But my wife might."

"She would if she has any sense at all."

The trooper turned his bike and with a wave of his hand roared down the pathway.

The doctor hung onto the door as Amanda's kicks landed on the other side.

"How are we going to keep her distracted?" Miss Cathaway asked nervously.

"If worse comes to worse, we can sit on her."

The doctor opened the door to receive Amanda's flying form in his arms.

"If we could just reason with her," Miss Cathaway wailed, struggling with Amanda's thrashing ankles while the doctor somehow got her to the sofa in the living room.

"Reason is for the reasonable," the doctor said grimly. Quite suddenly he had had enough of Amanda. Putting a knee across her legs, he released one hand and brought it down with admirable force on Amanda's hard little behind.

"Oh!" Amanda yelled.

"This," the doctor said, continuing the treatment, "is long overdue."

"Ouch! How *dare* you spank me! Ow!"

"Perhaps—" said Miss Cathaway, after a few more whacks.

"You stay out of this," the doctor said.

Amanda fought, thrashed, and, once, when Miss Cathaway foolishly had relaxed her guard, bit.

"Hang onto her hands, but keep them apart and away from her face. Amanda, I'm tired of spanking you. Either you quiet down or I'll give you an injection that will subdue you for the rest of the day."

But Amanda was past hearing. Unable to break the double hold on her, she was lashing out in an alarming fashion, and was alternately sobbing and screaming out of sheer frustration. Her face was crimson.

"I think I'd better give her a sedative, anyway," the doctor said. "Call Mrs. Little."

"I can help you," Miss Cathaway said.

"I know. But you can't hold her alone, and she'll cut loose the moment I release her to get my bag."

"Mrs. Little," the governess called, panting slightly, as Amanda was making a final thrust for freedom.

For a moment it looked as though Mrs. Little either hadn't heard or wouldn't come. But finally she appeared, wiping her hands on her apron. She took in the situation at a glance. "What can I do?" she asked approvingly.

"Hold her here." The doctor relaxed his hold on Amanda's legs as the housekeeper took his place.

Amanda fought like a pack of panthers, but the doctor finally got the shot in and, against her will, her limbs stilled. She lay sobbing quietly, grief and anger on her face. After a while she went to sleep.

"It's terrible to do that to a child," Miss Cathaway said, desolately. "I must have failed dreadfully to have made it necessary."

"Don't take everything on yourself," the doctor said irritably, not altogether liking what he had done. "Plenty have failed before you."

Amanda was out most of the day. The doctor had carried her upstairs, and when she came to she contented herself with glaring at Miss Cathaway every time the governess went into her room to see if she was all right.

"You'll be sorry," Amanda once said ominously, before she threw the peanut butter and jelly sandwich Miss Cathaway had brought onto the floor.

"I am now." The sandwich had come apart and had distributed itself, mostly face down, over the rag rug. Gingerly the governess picked it out of the rug, which would now have to be washed.

"You'll be sorrier than that."

"Don't make threats, Amanda," Miss Cathaway said, and realized immediately that she had made a tactical error. Amanda's eyelids were a little heavy from the sedative, but her steady stare was as unnerving as ever.

When Miss Cathaway next went up Amanda was in her pajamas and sound asleep, her thin little body lying across the bed.

The governess stood looking down at her for a minute, pondering. The black hair lay in tangles around her head. The lips, so often narrowed, were now relaxed, indented at the corners. The shadow of a frown lay between the straight brows, giving the face a bewildered look. It seemed incredible that such fury could occupy that childish countenance when awake.

Miss Cathaway tiptoed over to the dresser and returned with Amanda's comb and brush. Gently she unsnarled the hair and brushed it so that it lay straight and smooth, a match for the half circles of lash fringing the lids.

"Amanda, you're almost beautiful." Her own voice startled the governess. Amanda stirred and turned her head. Miss Cathaway held her breath. But her ferocious charge didn't wake up. The governess pulled the bedclothes over her and tiptoed out.

chapter eight

It was still dark when Amanda woke up, angry and fully alert. Both her watch and her bedside clock were broken and her father, after many warnings, had finally refused to have them mended again. It didn't inconvenience her too much because she had an uncanny sense of time. At the moment, because of the sedative, it was thrown off. But she lay quite still for a few minutes until she got it back. After a while she knew it was about four. Without hesitation, she threw back the covers and found her jeans and sweater where, dopey as she had been, she had carefully hung them on a hook in her closet so that Tedious Cathy wouldn't put them away. Then, holding her sneakers, she crept downstairs, avoiding all the spots that creaked. Halfway down, as though in approval, the mariner's clock in her father's study chimed four. Silently she got out of the living-room window and across the porch and gravel. Then she put on her sneakers and flew down to the cottage by the light of a waning moon and the stars.

Leave your supper and leave your sleep,
And join your playfellows in the street.

rang through her head, beating to the time of her feet.

Normally, she was afraid of the dark, though she wouldn't have admitted it to anyone. But right now she was more afraid of something else: that Malcolm might have gone before she had had time to make him take her with him, to make him *want* to take her. Something on Malcolm's face when the trooper walked in told her that he wouldn't be around long. Maybe some of those stories he had told her about pot and peddling and money changing hands on street corners that she had only half-believed were true after all. Maybe he was training to be a tsar of crime, not a composer. Maybe . . . She arrived, panting, at the cottage.

She didn't even bother to knock. She walked in. Here the darkness was complete and thick. She stood still, waiting for it to lessen. A light would be visible for miles even with the curtains drawn.

"Malcolm," she whispered.

The echo came back from the walls. It was cold and her teeth started to chatter. "Malcolm," she said, louder, and then tentatively, "Manuel."

By this time she could see the shape of furniture and she went quickly to the bedroom. The bed was unmade but empty. There was no one there, or in the kitchen, bath, or closets. And there were no clothes hanging up or in the drawers.

"He's gone," she said aloud. "He's gone, he's gone, he's

gone." Her voice rose. Despair enveloped her. She threw herself across the bed and the sobs came like breakers, one after the other. He had gone and she didn't know where to find him. She would never see him again. The pillow smelled of the stuff he used on his hair. The sheets smelled of him. She dug her face in as the sobs started to become screams. "Malcolm, Malcolm." They had done this. They had sent him away. Her father. Miss Cathaway. The trooper. The doctor. All their faces seemed to hover above her. That Thing, pressing on her stomach, started to burst out and her face contorted. She felt as though huge, merciless hands were tearing her head in two.

But something inside her, something very small but audible was trying to tell her something. She held her breath for a second as she tried to find out what it was. About to scream, she waited. The heaving sobs slowed. She pressed her hand in her middle. And for a brief flash of an instant she knew that in some way she had a choice: she could respond to this overwhelming need to scream and destroy, or she could call on all her powers to hold herself together, not to let what somebody else did split her open. And then she could think.

She lay very still. Her breaths came slowly, as though she had been drowning and were now safe. And then, for a while, she cried, the tears that had not come before, flowing down her face onto the sheet.

Odd bits of what Malcolm had told her started drifting through her mind: the drugstore and the newsstand on the corner of the avenue. The record store on the other side of the street. The diner—Tony's—where they sold chili and tamales. The one next to the record store where they had pizza. The subway stop. He had built that street for her, shop by shop. The shoe repair. The poster store with the psychedelic cards. The religious store with the rosaries and plastic statues. The grocery. Half an hour from Grand Central . . .

Amanda sat up and wiped her nose on her sleeve.

She showered down at the cottage, using Malcolm's towel to dry off with and rub her wet head. It was still dark when she ran back to the Big House, but the air was beginning to smell of morning. Thanks to Miss Cathaway's compulsive neatness she had no trouble finding the right clothes: cotton plaid suit, amber jersey, socks, her new loafers, and a small brown beret. Over her shoulder she slung a neat leather bag. The main problem was money: she had only three dollars in her purse. Well, she'd have to "borrow" some.

First Amanda took a flashlight from the hall closet. Then, with her hand over the light so that only a sliver showed, she approached the governess's room. Miss Cathaway's door was always slightly open (in case you should need me in the night, dear!—Some chance!) and her bag was a dark shape on the chair near the door. Carefully, so it didn't rattle, Amanda removed it to her own room, pushed the door almost closed and with the smallest possible light from between her fingers, got out the wallet and extracted from it the money, which turned out to be less than she had hoped. Closing the bag, she crept back and returned it to the chair it had been on. Miss Cathaway slept on.

Pausing only to stick out her tongue at her slumbering governess, Amanda then went down the hall to her father's study, carefully shutting the door behind her. She opened her hand so that the light came fully from her flashlight, and went over to the desk and eased open some of the drawers. First she took some notepaper and envelopes, then poked around till she found a receipt with her father's initials. Finally, from the bottom drawer she took some large paper scissors and silently cut the telephone wire leading to the extension on his desk.

She was about to switch off the flashlight when it fell on the framed photographs on the top of the desk. Buzz, Giselle, and Chuck on the deck of the *Pied Piper*, blond heads shining in the strong sun. In the other photograph was their mother. Amanda stared at it. Calmly she put down the flashlight. Oblivious of the danger in making unnecessary noise, she opened up the backs of the frames, twisting aside the little metal tabs, and took out the pictures. She tore them again and again into small pieces. Then she picked up the scissors, paper, and flashlight and crept out, leaving the shreds of the photographs in the middle of her father's desk.

With her loafers under her arm, she crept downstairs, cut the two extension cords there, hid the scissors under the sofa cushions, and slid through the window. It was getting light. The next step was the hard part.

Once more in the cottage, she carefully drew all the curtains and flew up to the attic. The typewriter had been a Christmas present two years before, and in a fit of enthusiasm after getting it, she had taken typing in school until it started to bore her. Now she wished she had persevered, but she did know how to use it.

Sliding a piece of the notepaper into the carriage, she slowly tapped out the message she had made up and perfected while bathing and dressing. After one false try she was satisfied. Her father's own typing was erratic, and it was entirely plausible that he would have typed this himself instead of using one of his platoon of secretaries. Then, taking out the receipt, she carefully traced the tri-letter squiggle that represented his initialed signature. Fortunately, her fondness for crime stories paid off: she made the tracing upside down with the paper turned around. That made it look natural. Then she folded it, put it in her bag, put everything away, and started for the small Island airport, halfway between the Big House and the village.

Amanda kept her mind steadily away from the pitfalls that yawned at every step. The plan demanded absolute boldness. If she wavered for an instant, she'd be lost, more lost here than anywhere else. Because she was on an Island and then would have no way of getting off. She resolutely kept her mind away from that.

But her heart beat fast as she pounded on the door of Ben Simmons' cabin beside the small hangar.

"Ben!" she yelled. "Ben—wake up. It's me. Amanda Hamilton. I have a message from my father."

The door opened. A blond, wiry young man was tying the cord to his robe. "For Pete's sake, what is it?"

Amanda's heart gave a surge of thanksgiving. Ben, most obviously, had one of his hangovers.

The job of pilot was the least demanding and the most boring on the Island. Too lazy to take anything more challenging, Ben piled up his savings and whiled away his boredom with whatever unsophisticated delights were available—mainly beer and girls. Since he was an excellent and meticulous pilot, only the sticky and puritanical made comments about his frequently puffy eyes and almost visible hangovers. But Robert Hamilton—who hired him— didn't appear to mind, so the grumbles were kept to a murmur.

In his condition, Amanda devoutly hoped, he would be too befuddled to ask searching and difficult questions.

". . . so Miss Cathaway left last night, and Father wants me to go to my aunt on the Cape. She'll meet me at the Boston airport."

He rubbed his spikey hair. "I didn't hear anything about this."

"It happened so suddenly, her sister getting sick and everything. So Father said he'd send this letter for you and she wasn't to worry. My aunt, his sister, will meet me at the Boston airport this morning, only she wanted me to get there early as she'd have to drive in from the Cape and she wanted to get back as soon as possible." The story was as full of holes as a cheese, but she counted on his not seeing them.

Ben rubbed his head again and wished he felt better. He had a feeling that there was something about this that was queer, but he couldn't think too clearly. Also, while technically he was the Island pilot, his salary was paid by Robert Hamilton and his wealthy employer had sent him on some pretty freakish jaunts at various times, including a lot of chauffeuring of his children. That was one of the things about the rich—distance meant nothing. *I have to go to Atlanta for lunch. How about dropping over to Paris for the weekend?* Like the whole earth was some private carpet. Besides, Ben thought, he had that new girlfriend in Worcester, only a hop from Boston. "All right," he grumbled and tried to stifle a belch that was rumbling up. He failed. His mouth tasted horrible. " 'Scuse me," he muttered. "Be back in a minute." Then he peered down at Amanda. "I'll just give the Big House a ring to confirm all this."

"Sure," Amanda said, depending on The Hamilton Manner to carry her through. "But you'd better hurry. My aunt wants to meet me at nine thirty, and she doesn't like to be kept waiting."

She heard him inside, pick up the receiver and dial. She held her breath and crossed her fingers. He dialed again. He must not call the operator. "I guess it's still broken," she called out.

He came back to the door. "What d'ya mean?"

"It was out of order yesterday afternoon. They said they were working on it. Something to do with one of the cables being broken."

He pulled the letter out of his robe pocket and read it again. Then he looked at Amanda. There was plenty of gossip about this wild kid. Nuts, most of the people called her, and waited hopefully for the day that the last of the Hamiltons would be carried off in a straitjacket.

"Please hurry," she said plaintively. "He'll be so angry with me if I keep Aunt Kate waiting."

Something told him he should put Amanda in his car and go up to the Big House to get this straightened out. "Where's your baggage?" he asked suspiciously.

"My aunt has lots of my clothes. I spend part of every summer with her, you know."

No, he didn't know. But he didn't see any reason to question it. The rich seemed to have total mobility. The rich, that's what he'd like to be. Go here, go there. Beckon, and people came running. Pack my bag, fly my plane, take my spoiled kid somewere. "All right. Wait by the hangar. I'll be ready in a jiff." He turned. Conscience prodded once more. He looked over his shoulder. "How'd you get here?"

"Mrs. Little brought me on the way to Early Service."

That figured. Pious old biddy.

Amanda had chosen Boston because she did indeed have an aunt on Cape Cod—her father's formidable sister—and to throw everybody off the scent.

When she climbed out of the plane she went hurtling toward the terminal, waving excitedly at a clot of people obviously waiting for a plane and yelling, "Aunt Kate, Aunt Kate!"

Making herself not turn around to see if Ben were following, she threw her arms around a tall, well-dressed woman who was on the point of walking back through the terminal. "Aunt Kate!" she shouted for public consumption. Then she slid around quickly to see what Ben was doing and with total satisfaction saw him climb back into the plane. Quickly she backed off. "I'm sorry," she said to the stunned woman. "I thought you were my Aunt Kate. Oh, *there* she is!" And she took off after another woman who had just disappeared through a knot of people.

After that it was easy, although it was a bore that she was forced to waste a day in traveling.

After she had shaken "Aunt Kate" things took—temporarily—a slightly sticky turn. Marching over to the shuttle counter she pulled one of the tickets from the dispensing machine and was filling in an entirely fictitious name and address when a big notice behind the counter caught her eye: BOSTON—NEW YORK $18.90 including tax.

Even with the money she had stolen she had only fourteen dollars and thirty-seven cents. Amanda was still staring at the placard when she noticed a pleasant-looking reservation clerk obviously on the brink of being helpful. That was the last thing she wanted. Quickly putting the pen back, she beat a fast retreat, moving around clumps of people until she felt safe. Then she walked more slowly and thought.

She could, of course, simply get on the plane since, she knew from experience, the shuttle fare would be taken on board and they would hardly open the door and push her out. But they would certainly notice her, and probably trot right along behind at LaGuardia to see her safely in the arms of her "mother" (and, incidentally, collect the fare). No, it would have to be the bus, which was a drag, because she would have to put off finding Malcolm—Manuel until tomorrow. But it couldn't be helped. And since today was lost anyway, she might as well enjoy herself and have a snack. But not at the airport.

Four hours later, after a ride into Boston in the airport limousine, a snack, a horror movie, another snack and a stroll through the Common, she presented herself at the bus terminal, looking over the people with a shrewd, critical eye.

If it could be avoided, she didn't want some snoopy ticket clerk asking her if she were "traveling all alone, little lady?" Because, if detective stories and movies were any guide, bus stations were about the first places the police would start checking.

After a minute or two she attached herself to a middle-aged woman who looked both kind and stupid and was plainly coming *from* a bus.

"Please," she said shyly, breeding and good manners in every syllable, "would you buy my ticket for me? Mummy told me when she knew she couldn't leave my baby brother to ask some kind lady to get my ticket for me. She was so upset, but she said I would be quite safe." The big, tawny eyes filled.

"Of course, my dear. How far are you going?" Amanda had chosen well. For all her matronly looks the lady was a spinster and sentimental about children.

"Just to New York. My aunt will meet me there." She smiled bravely.

chapter nine

Miss Cathaway, a small tray in one hand, approached Amanda's door in a state of mild concern. It was past nine. Amanda, an early riser, had not come down for breakfast, nor had Miss Cathaway heard any sound from her room. The doctor must have given her a stronger sedative than he intended. With her free hand the governess knocked on the door. "Amanda?"

No answer.

"Amanda!" The governess's voice was louder and had a sharp edge to it. "Please answer me."

Quite suddenly she knew Amanda was not behind the door; that she was not in the house at all. Fumbling for the knob, Miss Cathaway flung the door open. The room was as untidy as usual. But what made the governess's heart seem to miss a beat were the jeans, shirt, and sneakers strewn over the unmade bed and floor. Hanging in the open closet were the shorts that Amanda usually wore when she did not put on her jeans. If she was not in the clothes she never voluntarily budged out of from June until September, then she must—

A chill crept through Miss Cathaway. Turning, she went quickly down the stairs, still carrying the tray, and into the kitchen. Mrs. Little was finishing her own breakfast, lingering over a cup of coffee.

"Have you seen Amanda this morning?"

Mrs. Little did not look up from the paper that she took from the porch early each morning. "Nope."

"Mrs. Little, I know you're angry with her, but can't we forget that for the moment? Amanda's bed is empty."

Mrs. Little turned the page. "Well? Why are you in a state about that? She's often up and out early in the morning."

"I don't know why. But yesterday—I shouldn't have let the doctor give her that sedative. I knew it was wrong at the time. But the trooper said he didn't want her down at the cottage while he talked to that young man, and I couldn't think of another way to hold her. I suppose I should have tried—"

Mrs. Little closed the paper and looked up. "The trouble with you is, everything Amanda does you go into a tizzy of guilt about. People like you make me tired. You keep backing down and backing and backing till a baby of three can walk over you and tell you what to do and how you should feel. How can you hope to help a child like Amanda unless you know yourself whether you're right or wrong? Did you ever think what's going to happen to her? Unless somebody stops her, she's going to go on having tantrums until somebody gets tired and locks her up for good and all. I wouldn't be surprised if that isn't why she likes that young

hoodlum down at the cottage. She had a bruise on her face
yesterday. He probably hit her. Everybody else just keeps
scolding and walking away as though she were a freak. I
bet he isn't running around wondering if it's all his fault.
She isn't a freak to him. Just a spoiled rich kid who needs a
lesson."

Miss Cathaway stood transfixed as the words were
pounded home like so many nails. That they were true she
didn't for a minute question and habit being habit, she felt
guiltier than ever. But the fact remained; she had a funny
feeling about Amanda; that she wasn't just out on one of
her early morning sorties.

"I think you're right. But I also think something's
happened to her."

"What?"

"I don't know. But I'm going down to the cottage."

Mrs. Little got up. "I'll go with you."

Miss Cathaway was about to refuse the offer when it
occurred to her that she might need her. Besides, at this
point she could do with the moral support.

They walked down through the field together, Miss
Cathaway thin as a spike in her skirt, blouse, and cardigan,
her mousy hair showing unexpected lights in the morning
sun. Mrs. Little walked beside her, in her uniform a solid
cube of white against the vivid green of the grass. To their
left, bisected by the upper prow of the cliff, lay the sea,
misty as violet gauze at the horizon, like aquamarine silk
nearer where the sunlight lay in flat patterns.

After ringing and knocking for a while, Mrs. Little tried
the front door and found it was open.

An effort had been made to clean the living room. Soda
bottles were collected and stood by the hearth in a large
shopping bag, along with cigarette butts and papers. Even

with the door open, the room still had a stale, smokey smell. A few sheets of music lay under the piano.

"Maybe he's just taking a walk," Miss Cathaway said, knowing, somehow, it wasn't true. Emptiness filled the house.

"Maybe." Mrs. Little walked through the room to the kitchen. Miss Cathaway followed.

The garbage cans were overflowing and the floor was dirty. But someone had washed the dishes which were clean and stacked on the drainboard.

"Pew!" Mrs. Little went over and opened the back door and all the windows.

"Here are the keys," Miss Cathaway said, picking them up from the table. She turned and went into the bedroom. "No clothes, no suitcase." She looked into the bathroom. "And no toothbrush or razor."

"Flown the coop," Mrs. Little said, over the sound of water. She was filling a bucket she found under the sink. She added soap and ammonia and hauled a mop out of the closet.

"Shouldn't we try to find out what happened? I'm worried sick about Amanda. I can't help feeling she's . . ." Miss Cathaway's voice trailed off. She couldn't bring herself to give words to the conviction that was growing in her mind.

"Gone with him?" Mrs. Little finished for her, not being hampered by such incapacity. "I wouldn't be surprised."

"You don't seem very upset."

"Why should I be? Amanda's your problem, not mine. Anyway, I've told you what I think." With a look of almost sensual satisfaction she lifted the soapy mop onto the floor and started attacking the dirty corners and edges.

Miss Cathaway watched her, envious of her gift of finding peace in practical accomplishment. It must make life a lot easier, she thought. And then she scolded herself: it's no use standing here mooning. I must find Amanda.

She started to leave the room. Without breaking her stroke Mrs. Little said, "You might begin with the attic upstairs. That's one of her favorite hangouts."

But Amanda wasn't in the attic.

For two hours Miss Cathaway searched, along the cliff path, through the woods, back to the Big House, down to the village in the car. No one had seen Amanda. Everyone seemed to cheer up at the thought that something might have happened to her. It made life more interesting.

Aware that she had lit all the fires of gossip, Miss Cathaway decided she might as well see Dr. Townsend, and went along to his office.

When he walked into the waiting room from his consulting room, she astonished herself by bursting into tears. The doctor went out and came back. "Drink this," he said kindly, holding out a glass and patting her shoulder. "What's that pestiferous child done this time?"

Miss Cathaway groped in her bag for her handkerchief. Finding it, she was about to close the bag when she paused, staring inside. After a minute she took out her wallet and opened it. "It's gone," she said.

"Your money?"

She nodded.

"How much?"

"About eleven dollars."

"When did you last see it?"

"Last night. It's an old housekeeping habit, figuring out what I spent during the day and checking what's left."

"Ummm. Do you know who has it?"

"I think—I'm afraid, Amanda. That's what I came to see you about." She drew a breath. "I think she may have gone away with the Delinquent. And I'm stumped. I don't know what to do next."

"Oh, Lord!"

"She said I'd be sorry," Miss Cathaway said thoughtfully.

"Are you sure she's not on the Island?" the doctor asked later that morning when they were back in the Big House. "She's spent all the summers of her life here, and there isn't one cave or hollow or shrub—and you'd be surprised how many there are, particularly in that belt of woods—she doesn't know."

"I can't be sure, of course," Miss Cathaway said wearily. "But she didn't put on her shorts or her jeans. They were in her room. And wouldn't she be wearing those if she were hiding out here?"

"What is she wearing?"

"I'm not really sure. I've only known her up here, and I've never even seen her in anything other than those playclothes. Of course—she has other jeans and other shorts."

"So it doesn't really prove anything?"

"No. Not really."

They discovered the cut telephone wires in the afternoon, when they tried to telephone the bus station in Potter's Bend, to see if anyone there had seen Amanda. Fortunately, an emergency repairman was available and dispatched immediately by the head office on the mainland to mend the lines.

It still didn't prove that Amanda was not on the Island. The only definite information they had of any kind was that Malcolm, alone, had crossed to the mainland on the ferry the evening before. Nor had the ferryman seen

Amanda at any time, although that didn't prove anything either. She could easily have hidden in one of the cars that were often ferried back and forth.

It didn't occur to the doctor or Miss Cathaway or Mrs. Little to check the Island airport.

"We'll have to call the police," Miss Cathaway said that evening.

The doctor rubbed his eyes. "Why don't you wait until the morning. She hasn't really been missing twenty-four hours. She hasn't been seen in the bus station or the ferry. She might still be somewhere around here."

"You really think so?"

He hesitated. "I think it's about fifty-fifty."

Miss Cathaway didn't. But she agreed to wait.

When the next morning brought no chastened and hungry Amanda, Miss Cathaway called the local police in Potter's Bend, pleading that the matter be kept as confidential as possible. "You know how the papers are about anything to do with the Hamiltons."

Then, after bracing up her courage with another cup of coffee, she telephoned Robert Hamilton's offices in New York and spoke to his secretary, Miss Peterson.

"Yes, I know about it," Miss Peterson said. "I was about to call you. Your local police have already telephoned trying to locate both Amanda and young Manuel Santiago— apparently he's been in some minor trouble down here."

"What kind of trouble?" Miss Cathaway asked worriedly.

"Nothing too much, unless they weren't telling me. Mostly they're looking for an old buddy of his who is in a spot—narcotics, I gather."

Visions of Amanda in an opium den rose before the governess's tortured mind. It would be just the kind of thing to appeal to her, "Oh, Lord," she said despairingly. And then, "What on earth will her father say?"

Miss Peterson's calm, efficient voice took on a shade of anxiety. "Well, to tell you the truth, we can't locate him, either. He's always given at least one number where he can be found. But not this time. When last heard from he was in London. He left there more than a week ago. But no one, in London, Paris, Rome, or anywhere else he has an office, seems to have the faintest notion where he is. It's never happened before." She sounded aggrieved and slightly disapproving.

Miss Cathaway for her part felt relieved. Let him stay where he is until we locate Amanda, she prayed silently.

The following morning Amanda was still missing, but Robert Hamilton was located. His Geneva office informed Miss Peterson that he had turned up unexpectedly from some Alpine retreat, and had been told of his daughter's flight. He was now en route across the Atlantic and would arrive that afternoon.

In the meantime the Potter's Bend police were confronting a very chastened Ben Simmons who, hungover and sheepish, flew in from Worcester and landed his little plane all but in the arms of two waiting troopers. He tumbled out his story. But when Amanda's aunt, Mrs. Hadley Martingale, was summoned to the telephone in her house on the Cape, she stated flatly that Amanda was not there nor had she been expected, and she herself most certainly had not been in the Boston airport for at least a month.

So the police turned back to Ben, who by this time was beginning to see that his new girlfriend in Worcester was going to prove very expensive indeed.

"I thought you said you saw her meet her aunt?"

Ben ran a hand over his wet forehead and tried to explain.

"You mean you didn't go into the Boston air terminal with that Hamilton kid and wait with her?"

Ben shook his head.

"Well where the heck have you been?"

As he stumbled out an answer, Ben mentally went over a possible list of job openings.

But the strangest part of all was that no one knew how to get in touch with Malcolm. The trooper had said he was simply instructed to ask Malcolm about a friend of his, Ignacio (Spike) Chavez, and that Malcolm disclaimed all knowledge of his whereabouts.

Was there a charge against Malcolm?

Not as far as he knew, but that didn't mean he knew everything the New York police knew.

In the meantime, the New York police were also trying to find Malcolm. But the Conservatory was closed for the summer. The Hamilton office knew only that he could be reached in care of his professor who was now on a walking tour in Europe, and Spike himself, on whom the police were trying to get evidence, starting the whole thing off, had disappeared also.

"There must be four hundred families named Santiago and they're scattered all over and keep moving from one part of the city to another. And trying to keep this out of the papers is forcing us to go about it the long way," the police explained to the infuriated Robert Hamilton when, tired and unshaven after hours of circling, he finally got into the airport.

He waited only long enough to talk to the police before chartering a plane to the Island. When he landed there he talked to Ben Simmons, fired him on the spot, rehired him when he realized he would have to return to New York, gave him a blistering tongue-lashing instead and went up to the Big House.

Stalking through the front door, he caught Miss Cathaway halfway downstairs and almost frightened her out of her wits.

"Where is Amanda?" he barked without preamble.

"I—" she swallowed, "don't know."

"Surely on an island with two women who have little else to do you'd think you could at least keep tabs on her."

"I'm sorry," she said.

The governess had had a severe shock. She'd seen Robert Hamilton only once before, when he interviewed her. And she had been so impressed with his courteous manner and fair good looks that when she got up to the Island and met Amanda, she had a hard time realizing they were related. So she was now as astonished as she was frightened when she saw quite a lot of Amanda blazing back at her from his face. But it was the burn of ice rather than fire.

When he heard her answer, any lingering hope that Amanda might have appeared from some unrevealed cover since he last talked to the police vanished. He threw his raincoat over the back of the sofa and started to walk aimlessly around the room, his hands in his pockets.

Miss Cathaway came slowly down the stairs, something that she had not really been able to define forming words and sentences in her mind.

Mr. Hamilton suddenly turned. "All right, now tell me everything that occurred before she left, down to the smallest detail."

Miss Cathaway had been over that in her mind many times, so she had no trouble complying. Amanda's father listened without changing expression. When she had finished he said, "So she seems to have practically lived down at the cottage. I thought I told you that she wasn't to go down there. I know I wrote her to that effect. I realize she's difficult, but couldn't you find something to keep her away?"

"No," Miss Cathaway said baldly. Mr. Hamilton was too well bred to be abusive, but something in his tone shriveled her. "No, I couldn't."

"I thought that after Miss O'Reilly, who seemed too disciplined, someone less—formally trained—might be better. Obviously I was wrong."

"Mr. Hamilton, you can think anything of me you like. My general incompetence has been attested to by almost everybody for years." The governess laced her fingers together to keep them from shaking. "But what were you doing in Switzerland instead of being here, where Amanda wanted you? That's what set her off. You told her you might not even bother to come this summer, with only her here. You'd go and see your other children instead." Behind her she heard the door open and heard the doctor's step. She saw Robert Hamilton give a curt nod in the doctor's direction, but he kept his eyes on her. "Go on," he said.

The doctor came in quietly and put down his hat.

Miss Cathaway took a breath. "You called her disturbed. I don't think she is, in the clinical sense."

"Are you a competent judge of that, Miss Cathaway?"
She flinched. "No. I suppose not."

"Are you?" the doctor flashed out.

"Perhaps not. But more than one governess, not to mention several doctors, have indicated that they thought so."

"And you were happy to hear it since it let you off the hook," the doctor said, surprising himself by the anger that was roaring up inside him.

"And what do you mean by that?"

"Please—" Miss Cathaway started.

"I mean," the doctor said, "that if you can write Amanda off as disturbed you can shove her out of the way in some school or institution, pay the fees, and forget about her."

"Who are you to—"

"PLEASE!"

Both men stopped, surprised. Miss Cathaway herself was surprised. She had never raised her voice before. But she had found what she wanted to say. "Amanda upset me terribly. She is far stronger than I am, and she can make a monkey out of me anytime she wants. But it would have upset me a lot more if I hadn't realized that in a way her anger is all she has. She doesn't have love. Where would she get it from? Do you love her?"

Robert Hamilton flushed. "Of course I do," he said stiffly.

"No, I don't think you do. Parents are supposed to love their children so you think you do. Actually, she irritates you almost beyond bearing, and she reminds you of her mother who deserted you."

He flushed even more. "She *is* like her mother, of course, but I don't think—"

"She's also like you. I never realized it until just now. But now that you're angry, even though you've got it all bottled in, you're very like Amanda. You look just the way she does when I know she would like to annihilate me. Only she gives vent to it. You don't. I'm not sure her way isn't better."

There was a silence. Then Miss Cathaway went on, "Before Amanda took off, she went into your room to get some of your notepaper, and before she left she tore to bits the two photographs you have on your desk—of your first wife and your three older children. I looked all over the room—even in the desk itself, to see if you had one

of either Amanda or her mother. You don't. What do you
suppose that tells Amanda?"

"I never saw any resemblance in Amanda to me," Robert
Hamilton said finally.

The doctor spoke. "I have. I noticed it this summer for
the first time. She also," he added drily, "has your high-
handedness."

"Now look, Townsend," Robert Hamilton began, and
all of a sudden instead of being frightened, the governess
wanted to laugh, because there was something about the
way he said it that made her think of Amanda, putting on
The Hamilton Manner. Only this was the real thing.

". . . I thought Miss Cathaway would at least be able
to keep her in hand, but it is plain that she was incompetent
to—"

"No, Hamilton. You look." The doctor stood up. The
smothered resentment of years rose in him, along with a
surprising protectiveness toward the governess. "Miss Cathaway is perfectly competent. What's more important, she's
kind. And . . ."

"No, Doctor, please." The governess, gratified, had
found courage.

"What I mean to say is," she began, trying not to sound
nervous, "if you put Amanda in some kind of a special
school or institution, only two things can happen to her,
because she knows that you will be writing her out of
your life. She can resist what they do, their theories and
therapy and impersonal kindness which she doesn't want,
and when she comes out, her rage will first destroy her
and then drive her back in—for good. Or she can yield it
up, and then she will have no emotion whatsoever. She
never will have. And she might as well be dead. I think,
and so does Mrs. Little, that she got along with that boy,
because he was the only person who didn't look down on

her or consider her as first of all a problem. I don't know whether he liked her or not. But he accepted her. Has anyone ever done that?"

Robert Hamilton's face was gray-white. He looked beaten. "No. I suppose not."

The door opened again. Miss Cathaway and the doctor turned and stared. An attractive young woman, somewhere in her thirties, in a well-cut suit stood there. She had clear hazel eyes with laugh lines at the corners and lovely skin. "May I come in?"

Amanda's father stood up. A little of the bleak look went out of his face. He smiled, rather ruefully. "Yes. Do. I can't—We need you."

There was a twinkle in her eyes. "In that case—" Her accent was English.

He waved a hand at the governess and the doctor. "Miss Cathaway, Amanda's governess, and Dr. Townsend. He paused. His cheeks flushed again. "My wife."

"So that's what you were doing when nobody could find you?" The doctor said with a smile.

Mr. Hamilton grinned and looked more human. "Yes. That's what I was doing."

chapter ten

After a restful, though spooky, night at the Hamiltons' dust-sheeted apartment on upper Fifth Avenue, Amanda got up early and sneaked out the service entrance of the building. Getting in the night before had been easy. She always carried her own apartment key in her wallet and all she had to do was to avoid Herbert, the night doorman.

She had managed to acquire a blister in her walk around Boston in her new loafers, and had meant to put a Band-Aid on it. But she remembered it the next morning only when she was in the subway going down to Grand Central from where she would officially start her search, but she wasn't about to turn back, and after that she forgot about it.

But several hours later she knew that Malcolm's casual comment—*half an hour from Grand Central*—covered a lot of territory. After reaching Grand Central Terminal, she crossed to the Uptown Side and got into an Express train.

For a moment, when she had pushed a dollar bill under the grill of the change booth to get a token, she had considered asking the man in it where a half hour's ride would take her. But at the last moment, she remembered all the useful things she had learned on television, put her head down, and mumbled, "One, please."

"What?" the man in the booth said. "Can't hear you."

Amanda raised her head but turned it away. "One, please," she said over her shoulder.

"Speak up, girlie. I'm here, not there."

Amanda put on The Hamilton Manner and glared at him. "ONE, please."

She didn't have a watch, of course, so once she got in the train she had to concentrate on marking out in her mind what seemed half an hour. But it didn't come to her as easily in the unfamiliar surroundings of a crowded, hot subway. But she was enormously cheered that a lot of the English-speaking passengers had cleared out by the second stop, and most of what she heard around her was staccato-quick Spanish. It didn't sound exactly like the Spanish that Malcolm—Manuel, she liked that name much better—had spoken to her on the one or two occasions when he was feeling obliging. However, it brought to mind the fact that the sooner she learned it now the better. She was concentrating on listening so hard, that when the train screeched to a stop and most of the passengers got out, she was caught unawares, and had no idea how much time had passed.

"What time is it?" she hastily asked one woman.

The woman smiled but shook her head.

"*La muchachita pregunto qué hora es?*" her companion, a younger girl, translated as they fought their way to the door.

"Ai." The woman smiled again and showed her wrist-watch. Thirty-five minutes had passed. Quickly, as the doors were shutting, Amanda got out. Coming out of the subway, she entered another world.

The people on this street were smaller than Malcolm and most of them were darker, but in every other way it seemed just the way he described. There was an alive, electric atmosphere that was part of the heat, the noise, and people hurrying, standing, talking, bumping into each other, and talking in the same high quick Spanish she had heard in the train. The street had a definite smell of spicey hot food and Amanda remembered that she had had no breakfast. Her stomach gave a great rumble of protest and desire. She looked around. A few feet away from her, a Popsicle wagon was doing a brisk business. Amanda went up, bought two Popsicles and walked slowly along the street, eating one.

Over the next several hours she walked up and down a lot of streets looking for one where there was a record store next to a card store where they sold psychedelic cards and far-out posters, and where across the street there was a diner named Tony's that sold chili and tamales. There were a lot of diners selling chili and tamales and a few of them were named Tony's. There were also a lot of record stores with marimba and Spanish music and hard rock blaring out of loudspeakers, and young kids inside in jeans and miniskirts, with black hair piled high or halfway down the back. She was quite sure that Malcolm—Manuel—must know some of them, and she wanted to go into one of them and ask if anybody there knew Manuel Santiago.

But it really wasn't any use doing it until she found the street with the exact combination of stores as he described them. Also, she was feeling a little shy. She knew she looked different, and she felt that everyone who noticed her, and lots seemed to because they looked directly at her, knew who she was. Of course, people in Potter's Bend knew she was different, too. But the way she was different there was something she was used to: She was a Hamilton, more slowly, it was different-different here.

It was hot, very hot. She had forgotten, if she ever knew, how hot it was in the city in July, because, now that she came to think of it, she always left for the Island immediately school was out—that is, when she happened to be in one of her numerous schools. Other times, of course, she had lessons from a governess at home and then she went up to the Island the first week in June. Anyway, she'd never felt, or smelled heat like this. It seemed to come out of the sidewalks and the brick walls and doorways, and there were little patches of tar in the street that were soft.

And there were other smells mingled with the spicey ones that weren't as pleasant. Amanda's nostrils arched a little and she found herself thinking of the mounds of garbage in the kitchen back in the cottage. That was what it smelled like, and she noticed that it got worse when she passed some of the overflowing garbage cans lined up outside the doorways. It was from inside the doorways that the food whiffs came. Many of the doors were propped open and she could see narrow stairways leading up dark stairwells. Sometimes there were women or men seated on chairs outside the doors on the sidewalk, which seemed to Amanda very strange, but nice, she decided. You could keep tabs on the action.

As the day wore on the heat seemed to mount. At some point, Amanda stopped for a while in a small park. Her blister was burning, so, noticing children wading around a shallow pool, she took off her loafers and socks and waded also. The water stung the blister so badly she caught her breath. Vaguely she looked around for a drugstore to get a Band-Aid. But she couldn't see one, so she sat on a bench till her feet dried. A hot-dog vendor passed and she bought one. But either she wasn't as hungry as she thought or it was too strong, because after two bites she lost all interest in it. She wrapped it up in the paper napkin and aimed it at the litter basket. It missed. She sat there looking at it, feeling strangely tired. A dog came bouncing over, pulled the paper off and started nibbling the meat. "You'll get a bellyache," Amanda said. But he ignored her, finished the hot dog, mustard and all, and wandered off.

It was when Amanda got up that she realized how much her foot hurt. A subway station yawned invitingly. But she thought hard about Malcolm and limped across the park to the next street.

As the afternoon wore on and the heat seemed to mount she walked more slowly. After a while she came to yet another record store. Inside was a crushed throng of teen-agers chattering loudly so they could hear themselves above the massive waves of music—a sort of Spanish rock that reminded her of Malcolm's, though it wasn't anywhere near as good—that beat out of the loudspeakers. Amanda stopped, hesitated, and went in.

Records were stacked everywhere. Record covers were lying all around. Amanda hesitated and for the first time in her life was aware of feeling out of place. Many of the girls weren't much bigger or older than she was, but they wore either miniskirts or jeans, and Amanda realized that the suit and beret and neat loafers that were so acceptable and invisible for traveling, now made her stick out a mile as the visiting square. Her dirty jeans, jersey, and sneakers would have been perfect. Nobody paid any attention. They were all busy talking to one another in lightning Spanish, shrieking with laughter, swaying to the music.

She picked out a girl about her size in jeans and white shirt, with hair as black as her own, but curly and tied in a ponytail. Around the slender tan neck was a thin circle of gold holding a tiny crucifix. She was busy reading the back of a record cover and therefore, for the moment, not talking.

"Hi," Amanda said, easing past a boy with sideburns and a tentative beard.

The girl looked up. "Hi," she said indifferently.

"I'm looking for a street with a record store next to a psychedelic store with groovey cards and posters and a place across the street named Tony's that has chili and tamales. Is it around here?"

The girl stared. "There are record stores on this street and the next and the next, and sometimes there are card stores, too. Also diners with chili and tamales. Why don't you look?" She had a strong Spanish accent, far stronger than Malcolm's—Manuel's. She also sounded hostile.

Amanda was tired. She decided that even though the girl was Spanish she was a drag. "I have looked. I've been looking for hours. But they aren't in the right order or I wouldn't ask you."

The girl shrugged and went back to reading the record cover.

"Thanks a lot," Amanda said loudly.

Everybody stopped talking. The girl slowly raised her eyes again. This time there was no mistaking the hostility. "You ask a question. You get an answer. Is there something else you want?"

The music roared and beat and then stopped in the middle of a note. Voices from the street chattered at a

distance. A horn blew. Inside the store there was no sound
at all. Amanda felt queer. Her skin prickled. There were
several snappy comebacks that came to her mind, but something else inside her was telling her very strongly not to
come out with them. Some of the stories Malcolm had
told her trooped through her mind. *We don't like foreign-
ers, strangers, coming in, snooping around.* . . . Only, of
course, she hadn't thought it meant her. She would be one
of them because of Malcolm, Manuel. She stuck her chin
out. "Yes. Do you know Manuel Santiago?"

Silence.

Then a boy pushed forward. He was short and stocky
and had on a red T-shirt and black jeans. "Which one?"

She was taken aback, then said pugnaciously, "Mr. Funny
Man. You crack me up. How many are there?"

He grinned, showing a broken tooth, and shoved a stubby
forefinger into his chest. "*Uno.*" Then he pointed to a boy
across the room and laughed. "*Dos.*"

A boy sitting on one of the counters pointed to himself,
grinning, "*Tres.*"

Another one yelled, "*Quatro.*"

Every boy in the room said he was Manuel Santiago.
The girls were giggling.

She had meant to identify Malcolm further as the composer who used the name of Malcolm Sanderson. But pride
burned up through her. She made a loud raspberry sound
to show she hadn't been put down and started out. Someone
laid a heavy hand on her shoulder, dragging her down.
Then there was a spate of Spanish and the hand dropped.
Amanda forced herself to turn, instead of running. She
stood in the doorway, her back to the street, her legs apart,
her cheeks flaming. The girl in the ponytail started forward,
but another girl, in a green cotton miniskirt put a hand on
her arm and said something in Spanish in a soft voice. The

girls around laughed, then the boys. The ponytail girl shrugged. They all turned their backs. Someone put on a record. The music started blasting again. It was as though Amanda were not there.

She walked down the street and concentrated on trying to think what time it was. But her head ached and felt slightly woozy. She wasn't afraid, of course, and she was very glad she had run away. But she wanted desperately to find Malcolm. He would be glad now to see her, even though, of course, he might not show it.

Amanda was also at this point very hungry, and she wanted badly to go to the bathroom. A coffee shop looked up at the corner. She went in and sat at the counter. Even though an air conditioner whirred noisily in the corner, the air was dank and hot. A strong smell of oil came from the smoking griddles.

Her hunger went. It was better on the street because at least it was open. But she felt too tired to move. And there was also that other matter that must be taken care of immediately.

A large dark man with bare hairy arms and a bandit's mustache came over and stood in front of her. "*Si?*"

Amanda looked up. Sweat was on his forehead. He was picking his teeth with a wooden toothpick and staring idly out the window.

Rather frantically Amanda stared around the room for the welcome sight of a door marked *Ladies*. There was none. "Do you have a ladies' room?" she said flatly.

He turned his attention to her, his brows up. "*Qué?*"

"Do you have—" Amanda started, realized he wasn't derstanding anything, and then did what No Hamilton Does In Public: burst into tears.

A gentle hand tapped her on the shoulder. "Come."

A large woman with gray-black hair and a kind face led

her back through the kitchen, into a hallway, and opened
a door.

"Thank you," Amanda breathed, and bolted in.

The little bathroom was not only spotless, it was relatively
cool. Gratefully, Amanda splashed cold water on her face,
washed her hands and dried them on a paper towel.

When she got back into the restaurant, the woman was
busy serving one of the tables on the side. Amanda waited
until she was through and then went up to her. "Thank
you very much," she said shyly.

"You eat something." The woman patted an empty table
and Amanda sat down. A glass of milk and a toasted cheese
sandwich appeared in front of her and with them her
appetite. She ate it without pausing except to swallow her
milk. Then with another smile, the woman took away the
plate and glass and produced a glass dish with two scoops
of chocolate ice cream. Those vanished. Old Cathy should
see me now, Amanda thought, licking the last of the ice
cream off her spoon. To her surprise a pang that could
almost be described as homesickness seized her. And Careful
Cathy didn't seem—at this distance—quite such a drag as
she had before. Not a drag at all, really. In fact, Amanda
thought, feeling sleepy, she wouldn't mind if her governess
suddenly appeared in the doorway saying one of her stupid
things.

Amanda made herself sit up. "That was great," she said
to the nice woman, who was smiling down at her. "Do
you speak English?" she asked, hesitantly.

"*Un poquito.*"

She could translate that, anyway. A little. Something
told her this woman wouldn't understand a long sentence
involving record stores and psychedelic cards. "Do you
know Manuel Santiago?"

"Manuel Santiago." The woman frowned and shook her head. She turned and fired some Spanish at the man, who shrugged.

She turned back. "No. We do not know."

Amanda sighed. Then she gave a tremendous yawn.

"Ah, *pobrecita*, you should sleep. Why are you here? You do not live here—no?"

"No." Depression descended on her. But it was still light outside, and she had to find Malcolm. She opened her bag and put her hand in for her wallet. It wasn't there. Hastily she looked down into the bag. Except for a handkerchief, a pencil, a ballpoint pen, and some gum, it was empty.

"My wallet. It's gone."

The man at the counter made a snorty sound.

"Be quiet, Pablo," the woman said. She looked down at Amanda. "You had it—when?"

"Today. This morning." Amanda went back over the morning. She'd bought the subway token. And the Popsicles. But she hadn't opened her bag for the pops. She'd put the change from the dollar bill she'd handed the man in the subway booth in her jacket pocket and used that to buy the ice cream with. She ran her hand into her pocket and found two quarters left. "At the subway station," she said slowly.

"Here?" The woman waved a plump hand out the window.

Amanda stared at the familiar railings and post of a subway entrance—of all subway entrances. "I don't know," she said.

The woman picked up the ice-cream dish and wiped the table. "You go home now. Yes? It is better."

"I have to find Manuel Santiago."

"Here? He lives here?"

"I don't know. He said thirty minutes from Grand Central."

"Ai—that could be anywhere. Uptown, downtown, the Bronx. Harlem."

"Downtown?" That had never occurred to her. But Malcolm hadn't said whether it was up or downtown. She'd just assumed it was uptown. "He didn't say," she said. It seemed much hotter all of a sudden. The band of her beret felt tight, so she took it off and rumpled her hair which was damp and clinging.

"He is a friend of yours, this Manuel Santiago?" Pablo had come from behind the counter and was now standing huge and formidable beside the woman.

"Yes. My best friend."

"And your name. What is it?"

Amanda started to tell them when she realized that she mustn't. Almost she could see the FBI men, fanning out, *Have you seen a picture of this girl, Amanda Hamilton? Her father is the international banker, Robert Stewart Hamilton. He's distraught and has offered one million dollars to the person who finds her. . . .* There would be her father, on CBS news, his face strained, his hands over his eyes. . . . *I never realized how unhappy I had made her, how brutal I had been. . . .*

"—Jane," she said quickly. "Jane—Smithers."

Pablo grinned under his ferocious mustache. "And I," he said, sticking his thumb into his chest, "am Pablo Picasso."

Amanda revived a little. "Funny!"

"Ha ha," Pablo said and pointed his finger at her. "You go home. Now. *Inmediatamente.* Is not good, you here. *Comprende? Mal.* Bad."

Amanda got up. It was still light outside, but it wouldn't

be for long. "I'm sorry about the money." She glared at Pablo but couldn't work up any real heat because he reminded her so much of Malcolm. Not in his looks. But because he was so gutsy. "I bet you think I'm welshing."

"*Como?*"

"You think I'm cheating you!" It was important that he not think that.

He grinned. "*Si. Naturalmente.*"

Amanda stamped her foot before she remembered her blister. It hurt. "It's not true. It was stolen. I wouldn't pull something like that!" Then she remembered the eleven dollars and where it had come from.

Pablo patted her cheek, then put his hand in his pocket and pulled out some money. He picked out a dollar, took her hand, and folded it around the money.

"I don't want your lousy money. I just want you to understand I'm not stealing." She flung the bill at him. It fluttered and dropped on the table.

There was complete silence.

Pablo picked up the dollar, smoothed it, and put it in his pocket. Then he turned and went behind the counter and picked up a newspaper. The woman shrugged, made a noise like "tsk," and moved slowly around the tables wiping them off.

Amanda wanted very much to cry, so she concentrated on thinking about being a Hamilton and what Hamiltons do and do not do in awkward situations. They did not climb down: that went without saying. But in this hot sticky kitchen it was hard to tune in on the right wavelength for that. Finally she decided that she should walk slowly out as though none of it had happened.

It was cooler outside, and the sky was beginning to be dove-colored. There were a few lights in some of the store

windows and even more people on the street. Amanda
turned the corner and started to limp along, examining the
stores for records and cards. Her foot was much sorer.
Walking over to the inside of the sidewalk, she leaned
against a store window and stood on one foot while she
pulled down her sock and examined her heel. It was bright
pink and the skin was peeling off. Gingerly she pulled up
her sock and put her foot down.

Some teen-agers, walking four abreast, bumped into her
and said something in Spanish. A man came up to her,
smiled and put his hand on her arm. Throwing it off, she
forgot her limp and flew back down the street to the
corner, flung open the coffee-house door, and hurtled in.
Two people were now sitting at a table over by the window.
Pablo was cooking something over the griddle. The woman
was talking to the couple in Spanish.

Amanda went over to the counter. "I'm sorry," she said
loudly. "Truly." Her throat hurt and in a second both her
eyes and her nose were going to run.

Pablo turned and looked carefully at her. Then he
grinned. "Hokay."

The woman came over. "You take money?"

Amanda shook her head. "No. I can get home on the
subway. See?" She pulled out the two quarters. She knew
now she would not find Manuel tonight. And because her
key was in her stolen wallet, she'd have to steal the doorman's duplicate. She knew where he kept his keys and she
would simply wait until he had gone to deliver a package
or get a taxi for somebody and go in and take it.

Pablo pulled out the dollar bill. "You take anyway.
Si? Like good girl."

Dimly Amanda realized it would be right to take it.
Besides, she needed to buy herself some dinner. "Thank
you," she said humbly.

After a great deal of thought, Amanda bought some corn Fritos and a pint of chocolate ice cream to eat at home. That left a quarter from the dollar Pablo had given her. Which meant that she had now seventy-five cents for tomorrow. Slipping past George, the other doorman, was not so easy. In mid-July not too many tenants in the big cooperative apartment house were in town, so he had a lazy time of it, gazing dreamily across Fifth Avenue into the park. And since George had known her since she was born, practically, she didn't have a hope of his not recognizing her. On the other hand, waiting at the corner, poking her head around every few minutes to see if George were busy wasn't too good an idea either. It made her conspicuous. Amanda was standing, clutching her paper bag, and racking her brains, when she saw a truck drive up on the side street and a man with some kind of a box get out and go down a side alley. On an impulse, she darted back into the alley, tore up to the door, and waited on one side of it. In a few minutes she heard footsteps pattering down the service steps. The door swung open. Without a backward glance to where Amanda was standing, flattened against the wall like a TV spy or private eye, he went whistling down the alley. As the door swung back, Amanda reached and caught the knob. It almost pulled her arm out because the door was heavy and the spring powerful, but she managed to hold it long enough to nip around and inside.

Once inside, she let the door slam, in case George was listening for it, and then stood still. "Whooo," she said softly to herself. Then she took off her loafers and tiptoed up to the first landing, deposited her paper bag and her shoes, and crept down. Pushing through the door leading to the lobby, she saw, standing out under the awning, George's broad back in the dark blue uniform. He seemed to be watching some children playing hopscotch in the waning light across the street.

It was a risk, of course, but one had to be prepared for them. Amanda took a deep breath, then ran on her stocking feet across the parquet floor of the lobby to George's office. The keys to the apartments were in a deep drawer hidden underneath a counter. Pulling it open, Amanda held her breath, because the drawer squeaked slightly, but she heard no sound. Gingerly she extracted the right key ring. Getting the key off was another matter. She didn't dare struggle with it down here. Holding the keys together so they wouldn't rattle, she gently closed the drawer, crept around the corner, and looked out. George was still watching the children. Amanda flew across the lobby and into the back area. Then she went upstairs, picking up her bag and the shoes on her way. On the third floor, she considered taking the service elevator. But she knew it made noises, groaning and wheezing. George would be certain to hear, and wonder who was using it. That was the bad part about it being summer. In winter there was so much coming and going he probably wouldn't notice. But in July, with nothing to do, he could hardly miss. So Amanda pushed the thought away, made herself think instead about Malcolm, and climbed up to the twelfth floor, with stops to breathe and eat some Fritos. The trouble was, they made her thirsty, and by the time she reached her own apartment, she was very thirsty indeed, and very tired. And her heel was one large burning pain.

Wearily, she staggered through the back door, closed and locked it from the inside, and then sat down on a kitchen chair. After a while she got up, found a glass in a cupboard, and drank two large glassfuls of water. Then she limped into the front of the apartment.

It really was spooky, all those shapes covered by dust

sheets. But she was too tired to care—far more tired than the previous night. She went into the nearest bathroom, her father's, and turned on the bathtub faucets, and as the cool water splashed and mounted, she got out of her clothes and climbed in. When the water hit her heel she gave a yelp. But she didn't get out. She just slid down and let the tepid water flow over her. Her hair was getting wet, but she didn't care. This morning was a thousand years ago. Malcolm. . . . She struggled to remember something he had said, because it suddenly seemed very important, but she couldn't quite catch hold of it. She started to slide some more and then came to spluttering, choking, and frightened. She'd heard of people drowning in the bathtub. So she sat up, washed with the clean face cloth folded over the rail, and got out, pulling the stopper up as she did so. Wrapping herself in a huge towel, she opened the medicine cabinet. Toothpaste, toothbrush, shaving cream. Razor, shaving brush. Lotion. Aspirin. Iodine. Iodine stung, but there didn't seem to be anything else. Amanda took it out and closed the little door. Underneath was another cabinet. She opened that and found some Band-Aids. The box said medicated. She didn't need the iodine. Gratefully, she returned it to its shelf, got out the largest Band-Aid she could find and put it over her blister. Then she put on her father's pajama jacket, taken from the bottom drawer of the cabinet, went into his room, and laid down on his bed.

In that fraction of a second before she went to sleep she remembered two things: she had left the ice cream in the middle of the kitchen table. By tomorrow it would be melted all over the floor. And she had forgotten to detach the apartment keys from George's ring and return it to his drawer downstairs. Then she was asleep.

chapter eleven

Malcolm was playing his guitar, which for some strange reason sounded like a drum beating irregularly in sudden spurts, which made it hard for her to dance to any kind of rhythm. "Don't play so fast," she said as she woke up. But he paid no attention, and she had been awake for a minute or so, staring up at the ceiling in her father's room, lying on his bed, before she realized that someone was pounding on the back door.

She sat bolt upright. Then, as the pounding went on, she slid off the bed and ran barefoot out into the hall, through the swinging door into the kitchen quarters.

"Who's in there?" bellowed George's voice. "I know you're there and if you don't answer I'll call the cops."

Amanda stood frozen with horror. George obviously had found his keys missing and was checking the building floor by floor. What had betrayed her was a gooey stream of marshmallow chocolate, trailing in a sticky stream from the fallen container on the floor over to the door and underneath.

There was another pounding. "All right," yelled George. "I'll call the cops." His steps retreated.

Amanda tore back into the bedroom, dressed in about two minutes, and, carrying her loafers, ran back into the kitchen. It would be a risk, of course, opening the kitchen door. George might have pretended to go and then come back, waiting to trap the intruder. On the other hand, fat as he was, he wouldn't use the stairs, he'd use the elevator, and she could run down the stairs and out the back door. If she went out the front, she'd have to use the regular elevator and he would know in a second.

She could hear the service elevator now, wheezing down. She flew down as fast as she could and was only two floors above ground level when she heard it thump on the bottom and clank open. Peering over the banister, she saw the top of George's uniform cap as he got out and pushed through the connecting door to the main hall.

Then she tore down the remaining steps and out into the alley, remembering to shut the door softly. Pausing only to slip on her loafers, she sped down the alley into the side street and headed off toward Madison Avenue. She kept running for good measure until she had reached the Lexington Avenue subway stop at seventy-seventh street. Then she felt safe. She also felt jubilant, because in all the scurry she remembered what had come into her mind when she was half asleep in the bathtub. The word "Chelsea." Malcolm had used it, referring to where he now lived.

She wasn't quite sure where Chelsea was—downtown somewhere, she thought.

"Where's Chelsea?" she asked the man in the token booth.

"Lower West Side."

"How do I get there?"

"Take this subway down to twenty-third street, then take a crosstown bus to Ninth or Tenth Avenue."

It was only when she was sitting in the subway itself did she realize how much her foot hurt. It must have swollen, because the whole foot felt tight in the shoe which normally was so big it almost fell off. Gingerly she lowered her foot to rest flat on the floor of the train and felt pain shoot up her leg. "Ouch."

Several people looked at her. No one said anything.

She had planned to walk across town to save the extra bus fare. But it was all she could do to get up the subway steps, and she thought it better to blow the twenty cents and ride.

She got off at Ninth Avenue. "Where's Chelsea?" she asked a woman who was waiting for the light to change. She was a large woman with a red face, black hair, blue eyes, and a pug nose.

"Here, lovey. This is Chelsea." A strong beery odor accompanied the statement.

Amanda put on The Hamilton Manner. "Thank you," she said coldly. Then she discovered that that didn't help her at all. Did she start walking north or south? She wished she hadn't been so haughty to the woman. The light changed and the woman started across. Not knowing what else to do, Amanda followed behind her. Then she cheered up. Ahead of her, chatting amiably in the street were several Spanish-speaking teen-agers shouting at each other, carrying packages to be delivered out of a supermarket. She started to walk down Ninth Avenue, looking east and west into streets that seemed as if they might qualify.

Chelsea, she discovered, was a puzzling area, very different from the section uptown where she had spent yesterday. Uptown it was all Spanish-speaking. She knew she stuck out like a sore thumb. But here, there'd be a street full of Spanish-speaking people followed by another street with absolutely none, where she knew without looking there'd be no record or psychedelic card stores. There was a huge building on the right that looked like some kind of a college. On the left, Puerto Rican stores, leading into a Puerto Rican block.

On an impulse she turned into it, and proceeded east to Eighth Avenue. Once there she knew she had done the right thing, because that avenue, for blocks ahead, was pure Spanish—stores, people, sounds. She was limping badly by this time, but it didn't matter. She was sure beyond any doubt that quite soon she would find Malcolm.

Much later she wasn't so sure. Her spirits had flagged. Her leg was hurting terribly, and she was walking with her heel out of her shoe. It was hot. She was thirsty. Worst of all, she was beginning to get panicky. Hamiltons, however, she told herself with every burning step, did not give up. Wearily she raised her head, and looked straight into Malcolm's face. He was standing on the corner of Eighth Avenue and Fourteenth Street, chatting with some boys about his own age.

"Malcolm!" Amanda shrieked, and hopped, skipped, and jumped on one leg up to him.

"Where the—?" he started, his eyes staring.

"I've found you. I've been looking all over. I've run out of money and my foot hurts like stink, but I guess you can fix it for me, can't you?" She gave him an ecstatic hug.

There was a low laugh among the boys. One of them made a comment and they all laughed again. Malcolm, his face pink, was thrusting Amanda away with both arms. "What are you doing here, Amanda?"

"I've come to be with you. I don't want to stay at home any more. It's a drag. I won't be in the way, really. Nobody needs to know. Honestly. It'll be all right."

She found herself talking rather feverishly because it was obvious, very obvious indeed, that Malcolm was not pleased at all.

"You stupid kid. You think you can barge down here like you owned me and tell me you're going to stay. Well you can just call your car and chauffeur and take yourself back to Daddy."

"I don't have a car, Malcolm. Don't say things like that. And I don't want to go back to Father. Besides, he doesn't want me to."

Malcolm was embarrassed and furious before his grinning companions. "*Vamos!*" he said, and gave Amanda a shove.

"No. I won't. I've been looking for you for two days. I don't have any money, but that doesn't matter. I stole some from Miss Cathaway, like you told me you did from your teacher that time, when her bag was lying around—"

The rest of her words were drowned in laughs all around. By this time, quite a crowd had gathered and were watching Malcolm, grinning. Comments in Spanish flew back and forth. Malcolm's face was very red. "Blow. Get out. I don't want to see you. What the— What did you follow me down here for? I don't want you. You're nothing but trouble. And your father'll get me in more trouble for this. Get AWAY." And he gave her a final push.

And then That Thing was out of her, pressing against her insides until she thought they would tear open her body. Screaming, forgetting her foot, she went at Malcolm. "You rotten stinking lousy skunk. You acted like you liked me. You—" Arms thrashing, she closed in on him.

The shouts and laughs arose. "Ay ay, three dollars on the

baby terror! Manuel—defend your manhood." He was half laughing, holding her off, jeering at her. His friends were hilarious. She wanted to kill him. She—

There was a sudden yank on her shoulders and she was wrenched away. A volley of Spanish in a feminine voice cut through the noise. The others quieted suddenly. Even Malcolm stood there, looking sulky and ashamed.

"You!" the girl said, taking Amanda by the arm and shaking her. "You must not behave like that. Come with me." And she led the sobbing Amanda into a doorway and up some steps.

"Now. Here is some water. Drink it."

Amanda was sitting on a chair in a tiny kitchen with brightly flowered paper on the walls. Flies buzzed around the screens in the open window, which looked out on a courtyard.

Amanda was crying more quietly but with a dreary desolation. A box of tissues had been put on the table. "Here," the voice said. "Now dry your eyes. Stop crying. You are not a baby."

Normally, anybody who had said that to her would be sorry, Amanda thought. But she didn't have the energy to fight back. She took a bunch of tissues, blew her nose, wiped her cheeks, and hiccoughed.

"Would you like some milk?" It sounded nice and cool. Amanda felt hot and dry. She started to drink the milk greedily, but lost interest after the first few swallows. "Could I have some more water, please?"

The water, cool with ice, was handed to her. She drank all of that.

"Now," the voice said above her. "What is all this about?" The accent was Spanish, but not heavily so.

Amanda looked up into a vivid oval face framed in black hair. The large eyes were a velvety brown. "Who are you?" Amanda asked.

"I am Manuel's sister."

"Florita?" Amanda asked, and then remembered that Florita was dead.

"No. Florita died three years ago. How did you know about Florita?"

"Malcolm said I looked like her."

"Malcolm?"

Amanda raised her eyes again. "Manuel, I mean. He composes under the name of Malcolm Sanderson."

"I see," she said drily. She didn't sound too pleased.

"Personally," Amanda commented, with a slight hiccough, "I prefer Manuel Santiago."

"Personally, so do I."

Amanda looked up and gave a faint smile.

"That's better."

"What's your name?" Amanda asked.

"Marguerita. Sometimes I am called Rita."

She and Amanda looked at each other. "Tell me," Rita said. "Why did you come looking for Manuel? He is my brother and I love him, but sometimes he is no good."

Amanda stared at the floor. "Well," she said slowly, and then stopped. Then she took a deep breath and told Rita everything, right from the beginning.

When she was through Rita didn't say anything for a while. Finally she sighed and said, "*Norte Americanos*—they are funny."

"Why?"

"Because—you seem to have so much trouble loving each other."

"I suppose so." Amanda struggled to her feet and started to take a step. A really bad pain shot up her leg and she sat down again abruptly. "My leg," she said, feeling slightly sick.

Rita came around the table, went down on one knee, pulled Amanda's shoe and sock off and stared. What was left of the Band-Aid was ground up in a red, blistery, bloody mess. "*Caramba!*" she said softly.

"I had a blister," Amanda said.

"You have the mother and father of all blisters," Rita agreed. "And now it is infected." She was looking at the leg. Red streaks were shooting up toward the knee. "You will stay here. Do not move."

She hurried out, and Amanda could hear her dialing. She's calling the Island, Amanda thought, and tried to struggle to her feet. Then she stopped. What difference did it make now? And anyway, the thought of the Island was like a cool bath flowing over her. She knew now she wanted to go back to the Island more than she wanted anything. She'd get into terrible trouble. But that didn't matter either. What did matter was that her father would now certainly send her to That School. Tears slid down her cheeks. She wiped them away. She wasn't going to have Manuel's sister calling her a baby again.

"Now," said Rita, returning with a basin, "we will bathe it."

"Do we have to?"

"Yes."

"What's that?" Amanda asked nervously, as Rita emptied some grainy-looking white stuff from a box into the water in the basin.

"Salts. Epsom salts. Now—put your foot in."

"OUCH!"

"Put it in. Now. Your foot is infected. This will draw the poison until the doctor comes."

"What doctor?"

"Dr. Garcia. Enrico Garcia. My fiancé." She looked proud.

When the doctor came he turned out to be a good-looking young man, slender, with finely molded features and hands. He was gentle and friendly. Amanda decided she would have liked him very much if she had not decided never to like anyone again.

"Does it hurt?" he asked with a smile.

"No," she said, though it did.

He looked at the foot and the leg, prepared a syringe, and said cheerfully, "And now we will put this where you sit down. Rita—we need your help."

After that was over he said, "You must have your own doctor look at it right away. And you must get to your own home where you can keep it up. Can someone come for you?"

Visions of George swam before Amanda's gaze. He'd send a taxi double quick, and then call the Island. "All right," she said. "It's Dr. McGee, but I bet he won't be there. He goes away for the summer. I like you better, anyway," she said, forgetting her resolve.

Dr. Garcia smiled. His dark eyes twinkled. "I am flattered. But I think your family would prefer you to have your family doctor."

"I don't have a family," Amanda said tragically.

His brows rose. "No parents?"

"You have a father, Amanda," Rita said firmly.

"He doesn't like me," Amanda said, and started to cry as a wave of self-pity engulfed her.

"Perhaps if you were nice and sweet to him he might," Rita said. "Did you ever think of that?"

"We men," Dr. Garcia packed his things into his bag, "we like our daughters to butter us up." He put out his hand and touched her face. Then he took a thermometer from his pocket and shook it down. "Open."

When he took the thermometer out, Dr. Garcia looked first at Rita and then at Amanda. "Now. You must tell Rita here whom to call. You must go to bed where you can be taken care of, and your doctor must see you immediately. Who did you say he is?"

"Dr. Arnold McGee," Amanda said wearily. Actually, the thought of her own bed was wonderful. She was feeling distinctly queer. "But I bet it'll be that lousy sidekick he keeps handy, the one who calls me The Monster."

Rita went out. There was a rush of footsteps coming up the hallway stairs and a burst of Spanish. Amanda recognized Malcolm's—Manuel's—voice and stiffened. Rita answered, also in Spanish. Then she started dialing.

Malcolm came in. "Look," he said. "I'm sorry. I didn't know about your foot."

"It doesn't matter." She stared hard at her toes, concentrating. Malcolm said something to Dr. Garcia in Spanish, and he answered. They talked in low voices.

Rita came back in. "He's coming down for you right away."

"George? The doorman?" Not that it mattered.

"No. Your father."

She stared at Rita, fighting the aching in her head. "He must have come home."

She smiled. "To look for you, perhaps. Even though you are a *mal muchacha*."

"To send me to That School," Amanda said, desolation in her heart.

chapter twelve

Amanda opened her eyes and stared up at the ceiling. It was very familiar, but for some reason she was surprised that it was that particular ceiling. "I'm on the Island," she said drowsily.

"That's right."

Surprise cut through the fuzzy feeling in her head. She glanced down at the foot of her bed. Her father, his elbows on the foot frame, was looking at her. "We had a time getting you up here, but we managed." He pulled the tip of his nose, which made him suddenly real. He looked older and thinner, Amanda thought, puzzled. Then bits of memory started coming back: his arrival in the Santiagos' kitchen, filling the doorway. First he talked to the others. Then he scooped her up, carried her downstairs over his shoulder and out to his car, and drove up to Dr. McGee's;

the repulsive cheeriness of the doctor's stand-in—"Hello,
Monster. Who bit you?" Another needle, a big car, an
airplane, and then fade-out, interspersed with disjointed
fade-ins: a bump, voices, being carried somewhere. More
voices, some she knew, some she didn't. Helpless indignation as hands undressed her, and more voices, singly this
time, saying "drink this" or "turn over."

"What happened after the plane?"

"We flew you up here in the Island plane that had
brought me down, and put you to bed."

"When was that?"

"Day before yesterday."

She thought for a while. "I ran away," she said. "To
find Malcolm."

Her father moved up from the foot of the bed. He had
on slacks and a gray sweater. His fair hair had darkened
with gray. He stood looking down at her, his hands in his
pockets. "You did indeed. You also managed to get blood
poisoning. How do you feel?"

"So-so." The scene with Malcolm on the street was
coming back in every grisly detail. Amanda's hand groped
under the pillow. As usual, there was no handkerchief when
she needed one. She had just picked up the foldover part
of the sheet when she found her father's, held out in his
hand for her. "Thanks," she said gruffly.

"You're welcome."

Amanda blew her nose with great thoroughness. "He's
no good. Even Rita said so, and she's his sister—not that that
means anything," she said belligerently.

"Oh, I don't know. But speaking of sisters, Giselle sent
you her love."

"I bet."

Her father sat down on the side of the bed. "Manuel

isn't so bad. You just caught him off guard. Boys embarrass easily."

"Is he going to jail?" Amanda asked hopefully.

"What for?"

"I don't know. But he left right after the trooper talked to him. He wouldn't let me listen."

Her father grinned. "That was pretty selfish. No, Manuel isn't going to jail. All the trooper wanted to know was where a friend of his was. Manuel just got panicky and hightailed it home."

"And he acts so tough!"

"So do you. I talked to him on the phone later. He sent you his regards and apologies. He liked you."

Amanda summoned the strength to make a faint raspberry noise.

"I thought," her father said slowly, "that we might have a talk."

"What about?"

"Well—us."

"What's to talk about?"

"I haven't been a very good father, have I?"

"Lousy," Amanda agreed, not looking at him.

He winced. "You don't pull your punches, do you?"

"What's the use? When I'm good you don't know I'm there. When I'm bad, you do, even if you hate me." She raised her wet lashes and looked at him. Against the pillow her face looked both very young and very old.

"I'm sorry," he said unsteadily. "I got—confused. You see, your mother . . ."

"Yeah. Mother was a drag all right."

"Amanda—you mustn't say that."

"Why not? Did *you* like her?" The young eyes were shrewd and probing.

"Well . . . at first. I mean, we didn't have . . . Sometimes people find they don't get on."

"You sound like some of those trashy books Chuck and Giselle used to read in the cottage."

"And I suppose you read them, too."

"Sure. Why not? She didn't like me either—Mother, I mean. She—" In her mind there rose up an old memory: the expression of distaste on her mother's face when she went into her room one night. Her mother was seated at her dressing table, putting on her makeup. She looked up and saw Amanda in the mirror. . . . It was so far back she couldn't remember how old she was. "She—" Amanda started again. Her throat ached. Her mouth was behaving strangely. "Go away. I'm tired," she whispered. She turned around and put her face the other way on the pillow.

"Oh, no." He burrowed in the pillows, pulled her up and held her against him.

"I hate you," she sobbed.

"I don't blame you." But he didn't loosen his hold.

"You're a rat-fink and a goon. You're the rottenest father ever. You don't love me. You don't even *like* me."

"I'm anything you say, Amanda. But you're wrong about one thing. I do love you."

"Then why don't you show it? You don't even bother to come and *see* me. You write me lousy letters telling me to be good."

He smoothed her hair. "Because I've been a rat-fink and a goon."

"You're worse than that. You're the *Establishment!*"

"Now that's too much! Goon and rat-fink, okay. But not the Establishment. I can't be that bad."

"Yes, you are. You STINK!" She ended in a muffled bellow.

"Amanda, you of all people will agree that adults can be stupid. I've been stupid. I'm very sorry. I'm not going to be stupid any more."

There was a short silence. "My nose is running," she said, after a while, "on your sweater."

"What's a sweater between friends?" But he picked up the damp handkerchief and pushed it under her nose.

"You know," he said, after another pause. "Dr. Garcia was very impressed with you. He said it took a lot of determination and guts to get around on that blister."

"That's nice," she said listlessly.

"Don't you want to have character?" He sounded amused.

"Not especially."

"What would you like to have?"

"I want to be a sex queen."

He made a funny noise. "Why?"

"So lots of men will fall in love with me."

"Well, you'll have to satisfy yourself with just one for the time being."

"Like who?"

"Like me." He cupped her chin with one hand and kissed her cheek. Her face went pink. Her eyes sparkled. She slid an arm around his neck. "Mmmmm." She sniffed. "Is that shaving lotion? The kind you have in your bathroom in New York? I liked that. I put some on."

"Well, you'll just have to adjust to a new kind. I got this in London."

"Did you swing?"

"What?" He was momentarily lost.

"London, Swinging London."

"Oh. Well, yes. You could say so. I brought you a present."

"Smashing! What?"

He took a breath. "A new mother."

"A WHAT???" she reared back.

He kept his grip on her. "You heard me. A new model in mothers. I think you'll like her."

"Well! If that doesn't—If there's anything I don't need it's a mother. Is that why you've been cozying up to me?" Her voice rose. She could feel the beginning of the storm.

He gripped her arms. "Now you listen to me, Amanda. I have two things to say: One: There's going to be no more of these bullying temper tantrums. If you don't like what I do or say, you have the right to tell me. But you'll tell me quietly and with decent observation of the civilities. I have feelings, too. Rudeness is a weapon I won't have you use. Whatever it is, I'll listen. But I expect you to listen to me with the same attention. Two: I love you very much. Don't twist away like that. I mean it. And I'm not going to let you forget it. As your friend Manuel would say, *Comprende?*"

She tried again to pull loose, but he held on. "And you're not going to run away this time. We're going to understand each other, here and now."

"I suppose if I don't do exactly like you say you'll send me to That School. That's what you mean!"

"No. That's not what I mean. I will not send you to that school—or any other—unless you force me to. The choice is yours, Amanda. Do you understand that?"

Curious, those words. They struck a chord in her mind. . . .

He released her. She leaned back against the pillows. There was silence for a while. She picked at the quilt without looking at him. Finally she said sulkily, "I hate women. I like men better."

"So I gather." There was amusement in his voice. "But hating women is like hating yourself. Because a woman, with a little help from the Almighty and the rest of us, is what you're going to be." He pinched her nose. "A woman, who is also a sex queen. With character."

"If you had to get married, why didn't you marry Old Cathy? At least I'm used to her. She's awfully square. But she's not so bad."

He leaned back against the foot. "I have an idea the doctor got there first."

Amanda stared. "Wowie! You mean with Cathy? What a panic! They're *old*."

Her father closed his eyes. "Please, Amanda, spare my feelings, to say nothing of my vanity." He opened his eyes and went on, "You know, your Cathy, as you call her, did a powerful job of telling me off when I came up here looking for you with blood in my eye. She was the first to break it to me that I was not the world's greatest parent. The doctor added his two cents' worth, too."

"What did they say?"

He paused, recoiling from discussing with her his feelings about her mother. His temperament, training and upbringing were all against it. He could not imagine doing such a thing with his other three children. But then the problem had not arisen. Bringing them up had been like breathing. Just as living with their mother and loving her had been as easy and necessary as breathing. But Amanda, for better or worse, was the child of a different mother, and because of his attitude toward her mother, even after her death, he had been to Amanda what amounted to a different father. He took a deep breath.

"They said, more or less, that I took out on you the fact that your mother and I didn't get along, because you reminded me of her. That's true. I suppose I was afraid. Afraid of being hurt."

"*Afraid!* Of *me?*"

He nodded. "Yes." Then he said suddenly, "You remember, when you were little, kicking that puppy? And I took it away from you?"

Her face tightened. He could almost see her retreat. He said carefully. "You were afraid it didn't love you. Isn't that it? You tried to make it come to you, show affection. It was still a puppy and didn't know you. But you were so busy wanting love you couldn't wait. You felt the puppy was saying to you what I—and your mother—seemed to be saying to you: that you were unlovable. So you kicked it. Just as I—in effect—kicked you. Do you understand, Amanda?"

She scowled, folding and refolding the edge of the sheet. Without looking at him she asked, "Are you still afraid? Am I still—unlovable?"

"No, to both. You never were unlovable. That's what I've been trying to tell you. It was I. And I'm too busy now trying to win you back to be afraid. I want you to love me."

Amanda opened her mouth and then closed it. She looked at her father. It had never occurred to her that the shoe could be on the other foot. It gave her a curious feeling of power, which, in turn, gave her a sense of freedom. Along with a yearning to give him what he wanted was a desire to withhold it. It was confusing. But the desire to give won.

"I do love you," she said gruffly.

He smiled. "Wrenched from you by torture?"

"No. TRULY!" She leaned forward and hugged him. "On a gut level."

"A what?"

"A gut level. *You* know. Like it's in the gut, man."

Light dawned. "Like in TV?"

She leaned back and grinned. "Like yes."

Then she said, "Where is she?"

"Do you want to see her?"

Amanda nodded.

"Then you call her. She's across the hall in her room. Her name is Helen."

"I don't think—" Amanda cleared her throat. "Oh, all right. Helen!" It came out slightly cracked. "HELEN!" she bellowed.

Her father managed, stoically, not to wince. But he couldn't prevent himself from saying, "You sound like a bull moose."

"In rut," Amanda agreed.

He gave up.

chapter thirteen

The woman who came through the door had neat brown hair, straight and swept back into a twist. She had on a dark blue shirt-dress and loafers. She looked both chic and simple. Amanda scowled at her.

Robert Hamilton, taking in his daughter's aggressive stare, instantly recognized the Distant Early Warning signals. "Helen," he said nervously, "maybe tomorrow, when Amanda's feeling—"

"I feel just fine," Amanda said.

"Then you might try smiling."

"Amanda doesn't feel like smiling," Helen said. "Neither do I. Why don't you go downstairs or somewhere and do something male and heroic while we sort this out?"

Amanda hadn't entirely bargained for that. "I don't want him to go."

"But I do," Helen said. "I prefer him not to see the more bellicose side of my character so soon after our marriage."

"I think," Robert Hamilton said, beating a retreat, "I have to see a dog about a man."

"Funnee!" Things weren't going quite the way Amanda planned.

After her father left there was silence. Amanda set herself to wait it out. She still suspected her father of making a fool of her, after all.

Helen came over to the bed. "Well, Amanda. We might as well get straight to the point. Which shall it be—war to the death, or peace? You choose."

That again. "I'm getting very bored with having to choose all the time."

"That's the way life is. And the more you want to live it on your own terms, the more choosing you'll have to do. Between us, it has to be you."

Amanda mentally sniffed around this and found it suspicious. "Why?"

"Because it takes two to make war and it takes two to make peace—real peace. If I chose either one, you could choose the opposite and cancel it out, and then this house would be like an armed camp, with everyone miserable and everyone a loser. And how long do you think that would go on? How long do you think your father would allow it?"

She paused, while Amanda digested this, and then continued, "If you choose peace, so will I. And I think, together, we can make a good one, for ourselves and for your father. If you choose war, I will take that, too. But I will fight with my own weapons. And my weapon will be to leave you absolutely alone. You may do just as you

please and it will be your responsibility. You can make
people hate you as much as you like. And that will be your
responsibility. And you can go on till you break your
father's heart, and that will be on you, too, because he loves
you. And what will you get out of it?"

Amanda, pleating and repleating the quilt, examined
Helen's strategy from every angle, and a grudging respect
stole into her heart. As a strategist, Helen was no slouch.
She glanced fleetingly up at her stepmother's face. It wasn't
beautiful. It wasn't even pretty, really. But it had—character.
No pushover. Amanda felt an unwonted desire to please,
which she instantly resisted. It could easily be a trap.

"It's not a trap, Amanda."

Amanda almost jumped. Her glance flew up again. Too
surprised to guard her tongue, she blurted out, "How did
you know I was thinking that?"

Helen gave a comradely grin. "I've been there, too."

"Well . . . all right. But I don't want you to get the
idea I need mothering. I don't like mothers."

"Certainly not. I'm not your mother."

Amanda eyed her warily. "And all this let's-be-pals is
for the birds. It makes me sick. I've seen some let-me-be-
your-pal mothers at school. They're embarrassing. Yuch!"

"Yes. They're pretty sick-making."

"You talk funny. Are you English?"

"Yes. And it's not funny. It's English English."

Amanda arched her nostrils and put on The Hamilton
Manner. "The rayne in spayne stays mainly in the playne."

Helen's eyes laughed, but she said seriously, "Quayte!
Amanda, I think you could be a great dramatic actress."

"Don't tell her that," Robert Hamilton said, coming
back in the room. "I don't want to have to comb Broadway
some day. By the way, may I come back in? Has the
entente been ratified?"

Helen looked at Amanda, who nodded. Her father strolled over and tickled her cheek.

"We had just decided," Helen said, "that I wouldn't be a mother or a pal. Amanda expresses nausea at both roles."

"Gross," Amanda said. "Both of them." She was beginning to feel tired.

Her father looked down at her. "So what's it to be?"

Amanda, for once, was at a slight loss. But she also vaguely felt the matter should be defined, so they all knew where they were.

Helen said, "How about stepmother? Like it is."

"Stepmothers have a pretty bad press," Hamilton said.

"Putrid," Amanda agreed. "Like in the fairy tales. Grimsville! Yowie . . . dig that pun!"

Helen smiled. Her eyes crinkled at the corners. "Where can I go but up, in that case?"

Amanda yawned and slid down into the bed. Then she opened her eyes and looked at her father. "Is Manuel coming back?"

"No. His professor is getting back from Austria next week and he'll let him have a room in his apartment. It'll keep your boyfriend out of trouble, I hope. He's not the rural type, I'm afraid." He watched his daughter's face closely. "Do you mind?"

She gave a massive yawn, partly to play for time, and partly because she didn't want her father reading her mind. Things were looking up. But, though she was angry at Manuel, she had not forgotten him. The sound of his name brought both pleasure and pain. One day she would see him again. She was quite sure of that. And then he would be very, very sorry. Or very glad. Or both.

"Not really," she said carelessly. She added to herself, *for now.*